In lieu of the traditional "review" I have decided to offer up these pages for you, the reader, to provide your thoughts, praise, criticism, downright hatred, or secret messages to future readers of this copy. But please, no spoilers. When you're finished reading, if you feel so compelled, jot down a note and pass the book on to a friend. When these pages are full... buy another copy!

Acclaim for Nathan Sutton's

Tower Grove Park

I0583390

Acclaim for Nathan Sutton's

Tower Grove Park

Tower Grove Park

TOWER GROVE PARK

a novel

Nathan Sutton

Mohawk Street Productions St. Louis 2013

Book design by David Jacobsen www.foxtrotimages.com

Edited by Brittany N. Beard

www.mohawkstreetproductions.com

"… Because the only people for me are the mad ones, the ones who are mad to live, mad to talk, mad to be saved…"

- Jack Kerouac *On the Road*

Tower Grove Park is a municipal park in the City of St. Louis, Missouri. Most of its land was donated to the city by Henry Shaw in 1868. It is on 289 acres (1.17 km²) adjacent to the Missouri Botanical Garden, another of Shaw's legacies. It extends 1.6 miles from west to east, between Kingshighway Boulevard and Grand Boulevard. It is bordered on the north by Magnolia Avenue and on the south by Arsenal Street.

-Wikipedia

Tower Grove Park

All dates occur in the same calendar year.

NOVEMBER 26

The weather in Missouri has always been known for its strong and extreme personalities and the past year had been no exception. Multiple tornadoes carved paths throughout the countryside in the spring, and the summer had been uncomfortably sticky, the type of humidity that would cover you head to toe in the time it took to walk from front door to car door. Jeans were unbearable even at night. Winter was sure to be long and gray, possibly even beautiful at times. But it was rare that autumn would be so short-lived. The tree limbs were stripped bare before they could turn from green to orange to brown, and a violent wind had made its presence known for weeks, St. Louis catching the brunt of it. Dead branches snapped off from their trunks and fell to the city's streets, power lines were threatened nightly, and the window panes of the old brick duplex on Arsenal Street would rattle incessantly. It was cold for November, noticeably below freezing, and the season's first snowflakes looked ready to fall.

Inside the duplex, the one-bedroom on the second floor, vintage wooden speakers vibrated back and forth. The base drum was pushing the limits of the subwoofer and the paper cones started to crack and fray under the pressure. A summer issue of *Guitar Player,* addressed to Mr. Ethan Atkinson, a Christmas gift from his sister, sat unread, but heavily used, beside the record player. Everything looked heavily used. The place was certainly lived in. Squatted in, if judging only by its looks. Clothes everywhere, unwashed and rank. Fast food piles in every corner and between the corners. Dishes on the side table, dishes on the couch, dishes on the floor. The smell of it all, the dirt and grime, was masked only by a larger, overpowering smell.   Gasoline.

The duplex was on the 4600 block of Arsenal, across the street from Tower Grove Park. Arsenal Street was the rough side of the park, the south side. The side tourists would rather not park on, if for no other reason than it wasn't as aesthetically pleasing as the north side, the Magnolia Avenue side. The north side was home to St. Louis's beautiful secret, the Botanical Gardens, and the architecture facing the park reflected the Garden's beauty. The north side was of a different pedigree. It wasn't made up of the duplexes and apartments like its dirty counterpart, where tree roots cracked sidewalks and lawns would go weeks without being tended to. There were *homes* on the north side. Homes with children, educated children, where families with morals and values spent the moments before bedtime with hands folded and heads bowed, deep in prayer.

But Ethan lived on the south side. And on 4600 block no less, which was on the corner, barely five hundred feet into the parks perimeter. Inside, along with weeks' worth of wrappers and soda cans and mail and other general trash, Ethan lay sprawled out beneath his coffee table holding a bottle of cheap whiskey. He was motionless, mostly, aside from his big toe which moved to the tearing of the subwoofer. Every-so-often he would slide his socks along the carpet, pulling his heel toward his ass. The friction from the weather and the carpet and the socks would cause the hairs on his pale, skinny legs to stand straight. This might not have occurred if he'd been wearing pants. But he wasn't wearing pants. He was wearing just a pair of white briefs, socks, a t-shirt, and some whiskey down the front of the shirt, which had settled there after missing most of his mouth.

Half naked and fully drunk, he stared up at the underside of the glass top covering the wooden coffee table. Spread across the glass were pictures of Maggie Patrick: as Marilyn Monroe on Halloween; full of curves in a bathing suit below a waterfall with Ethan by her side; white teeth from ear to ear in one Polaroid, puckering for the camera while holding the mistletoe in another. Some of the pictures were more recent than others but in all of them she was midwesternly beautiful and strikingly confident. He looked intently upon each photo, studying her outline – the freckle on her collarbone, her connected earlobes, her pouty lips – gladly willing to cut his hands and break through the glass coffee table that separated them if it meant it would bring her back. Back to the time he stood on the other side of the camera taking half those photos, back to the time when she wanted to take photos of him, of them. He tapped the glass, harder than he should have, daring it to shatter down on his face. The window panes rattled, warning him to stop.

The duplex was drafty, but being nearly a century old and in desperate need of a remodel, it was not only tolerated, it was also expected. A gust came in through the window casing and sent a chill across Ethan's body. He covered his nipple with a forearm and rubbed repeatedly. On the last up and down motion his wrist pushed the chain of his necklace into his skin and he stopped. Reaching into the shirt he grabbed the necklace and took its pendant in his hand, squeezing it and pushing its imprint into his palm, and when it finally found bone beneath the flesh, he stopped. The pendant, a ring, an antique engagement ring, had created a white circle in his palm. Ethan stared at the circle until the blood returned and his hand showed no mark.

He struggled for a moment with the chains clasp until his fingernail was able to catch long enough to unhook one end from the other. Closing his right eye, he held the ring in front of his left until the ring framed Maggie's face in a particular photo. When she was happily in focus, he'd move to the next.

He pulled from the whiskey bottle, tilting his head slightly but not enough to keep from spilling. There was a rag on the floor beside him, and he wiped the mess from his face with it, cringing at how sensitive his upper lip and nostrils were to the touch. The pictures came in and out of focus. He was more fucked up than he'd thought. It didn't matter.

JUNE 1

The chair in his classroom wasn't anything special – four wheels, steel, green patent-leather, cushioned, full three-hundred-sixty degree rotation, and forty-five degree reclining capabilities – but it had formed itself to Ethan's ass over the years and the result was bordering on comfort. He had grown accustom to its charms. The chair had certainly aged and was in need of a healthy squirt of WD-40. Whenever he would recline the full forty-five degrees, it creaked loudly, every single time. His students would be taking a test, or reading from texts books, and Ethan could relax, then recline; the chair would creak and moan and inevitably disrupt the silence, causing each student to pop their preteen faces toward the direction of the chair. Over the years he developed a stern face to counteract the distraction, one that said, *It's just the chair, you've heard it before. Now, get back to work.* The truth was it made him laugh. Each time, without fail, all of their tiny necks would jerk their tiny heads straight into the air, like they were all attached to the same string.

There were no tests on this day, the first of June, not this late in the year. Today, in the last hour, on the last day of school, the kids were packing up supplies, signing yearbooks, and talking amongst themselves; talking loudly, at that. There were banging against desks, chairs screeching against the floor, one clique talking louder than the next; controlled chaos. But the same way a man can fall asleep on a busy city bus, Ethan allowed their voices to blend into a calming, white noise effect, and he was able to relax. After all, the year was as good as done.

He looked out the long row of windows that formed the top half of the wall along the school's east wing. Though he'd never had a class in the western wing, he could tell by walking through the halls, visiting fellow teachers, or just plain killing time, that he preferred the east wing over the west wing. The east brought the sunrise, the sunrise brought energy, and that energy made it easier to get through the morning classroom routine. By midday, the sun was shining on the other side of the school, out of sight, signifying his works completion. On some level, at least in Ethan's mind, this simple east side feature made the work day breeze by much quicker than it would say, if the building had been directed at another angle, or perhaps, if he taught class over in the west wing. On the west wing, he assumed, the afternoon sun would mock him through the windows, beckoning him to come out and play, to experience the outdoors instead of being trapped inside a school house, with children. *Come, enjoy the freedom of adulthood, frolic!* There was none of that mockery from his eastern wall of windows; just a good morning greeting, the raising of two coffee cups, his and the sun's, a mutual respect.

Reclining and looking out the window on a clear day, such as it was that afternoon, Ethan felt he could see the country's entire sky. From Portland, across St. Louis, to Washington D.C.: a

10

perfect blue, too perfect. Even the clouds themselves looked like a painting one might see hanging in the lobby of a Holiday Inn, fluffy and white, like unraveled balls of cotton. Ethan's mind drifted through the window, out past the lawn where the kids would play during recess, and into the blue sky, where it settled on one of the perfectly brush-stroked clouds, and began to play. He got lost in the cloud, which was no longer a cloud, but rather, a bird; a small bird in a big cloud in a bigger blue sky, a sky that stretched from one end of the window wall to the other, from Pacific to Atlantic. The bird floated slowly, calmly through the air, like a slow motion montage, begging to be reflected upon, and admired. But it didn't last. The bird must have been painted with water colors because as it flew past Ethan, its beak and wings began to wash away, fading into the sky. Like drops of blood in a tub of water, the bird gave way to the blue sky, losing itself to become one with something bigger.

"Mr. Atkinson? Mr. ATKINSON!?" one of the students voices called.

The sound of his name ripped him out the sky and back into the classroom, into his creaky old chair, and the voices of eleven seventh graders combined into one, powerful, disruptive noise. The same peaceful sound that had helped transcend him into the clouds just minutes before had transformed instantly into *noise*. He could hear individual voices, specific laughter, shouting, nails running down the chalkboard of his ears. Their young voices now sounded like an awful band, with an offbeat drummer and aggressive distortion.

"Mr. Atkinson?" said voice said again. When he turned, Ethan saw that it was Jacob, one of his second year students.

As he looked into his eyes, Ethan tried to remember what it was like to be that age, to look up to someone, rather than judge everyone. He liked Jacob more than some of the others. Of course he liked everyone equally, but Ethan was still human, he had his

11

favorites, and Jacob was one of them. He was eager to learn and his handicaps were subtle, manageable, in comparison to many of the other special education kids. Ethan had been tutoring Jacob in math and science for the past several months and they'd formed a bond that most student-teacher relationships would never have the chance to earn.

Ethan thought of Mr. Rathner, his own math tutor back when he was in grade school. Ethan struggled with algebra when he was young, twelve or thirteen years old, and Rathner helped him push through. When it came to sports, Ethan excelled as a child, he was fast and could run like the wind, but this new brand of math, solving X with Y, was a difficult hurdle, and it often slowed him down. Thankfully, Mr. Rathner was a brilliant tutor. He seemed to have something personal at stake when it came to Ethan's success. When Ethan couldn't wrap his head around the problem, Rathner never gave up. And when the light finally came on – the Light Bulb Moment, as Mr. Rathner dubbed it – they would both join in celebration. As a tutor, Mr. Rathner made it fun, he brought the problem out of the book and into real life, making everything tangible, and together they conquered algebra. Nearly two decades later, Ethan still thought of Mr. Rathner, wishing there was some way to contact the old man, wondering if he were even still alive, so he could thank him for the pride and confidence he'd instilled.

Ethan hoped Jacob shared similar feelings toward him. Jacob was a good kid, a strong minded kid, and though he had autism, he never used it as an excuse to slack off or quit on an assignment. To Ethan, Jacob would fight against the things that were holding him back, rather than give in and fold like most people do when the odds aren't stacked in their favor. It was that kind of courage, that backbone, that middle-finger in the face of adversity, which the special education students showed daily. And Ethan couldn't help but be affected. Their inner strength inspired him, and as long as it continued to do so, he would teach with all he had to give, and nothing less.

"Can you sign my yearbook?" Jacob asked, pen in hand, once he had Ethan's attention.

"Of course," Ethan smiled as he took the book. He paused for a moment, thinking of something brilliant to say, but nothing was readily available. Suddenly, feeling embarrassed that the perfect words weren't ready to fall out of his fingertips, Ethan started to scribble the first thing that came to mind.

Have a great summer. Read a book. Smile. Mr. Atkinson.

Awful, he thought to himself. Mr. Rathner would've known precisely what to say.

Jacob sat down, simultaneously happy to receive his favorite teacher's signature, yet dissatisfied with the lack of inspiration and the impersonal message.

The chair creaked as Mr. Atkinson stood up to address his students.

"I've got one more assignment for you all before you pass my class." He said it with a wink (all but one of his students would be returning in the fall, as the special education program at Park View Elementary was more of a running mentorship program, a guide to help the students apply what they learned during regular coarse work). His joke was met with a collective groan, a moan really; like he'd just crushed a bag full of puppies.

"I want you all to write for five minutes," Ethan said. "That's all, just five. The last five minutes of the year and then you're free. Pull out a notebook, or a piece of scrap paper; whatever you got left in there, and a pen. I want it in ink." He smiled and raised a brow at the boy in the front row. "Tell me one thing you learned in the past nine months. And then, in your wildest dreams, with all of your imagination, tell me what you want to do this summer. Don't hold back. Money isn't an object;

nothing can hold you back except your own brain power.
Whatever you want, write about it, okay? It just might happen."

He looked over the class once more, they were quiet, they were writing. He walked back to his desk and sat down. The chair creaked. Eleven tiny heads quickly popped up.

JUNE 18

A warm breeze shot through the screen door and blew the pleasant smell of barbeque around the kitchen. The previous day's storm brought on a cold front, chilling the air outside and providing quite the pleasant summer evening. Temperatures had been on a bit of rollercoaster the past few months, which wasn't uncommon for the Midwest. May saw record highs and foretold a difficult summer, but the first few weeks of June were unbelievably mild. In fact, they were so mild that Rachel Montgomery, Ethan's only sister, decide to kill the air-conditioner inside her and her husband's house, and open all the windows instead. It was comforting for Ethan, picturesque even, to watch the white curtains inhale and exhale against the window screen. It somehow added a dose of simplicity to their family dinner.

These family dinners were more than some weekly routine. They were habitual, expected, and its significance was hard to label, at least for Rachel and Ethan, given their tumultuous upbringing. But it was, most certainly, significant. It was necessary, and it was never taken for granted. For years, even before Rachel and Winslow, became Mr. and Mrs. Montgomery, the group would instinctively set aside at least one evening per week to break bread, connect with one another, and scrape together some sort of fulfillment from their otherwise hectic and busy schedules. The event was also exclusive. Back when Ethan was in college at Saint Louis University, it was just he and his sister eating Chinese delivery in the duplex. Once things got serious with Winslow, he was allowed into the club, and delivery turned into home cooking. Next came Maggie, Maggie Patrick. Ethan had fallen in love with her before they'd even spoken a word to one another, so it was only natural, at least to Ethan that their first 'official' date would be at the family dinner. Sink or swim. If she could hang, if she could fit in and take a joke, maybe even crack a few of her own, and most importantly, if Rachel liked her, she could become part of the exclusive club too. If not, if she failed even slightly, well then, fuck her. Move on. But she didn't fail. She fit in seamlessly. She was the one, without question. Dinner for four. And when Rachel and Winslow bought their house on the north side of the park, the safe side, the family side, dinners logically moved with them.

The four of them, each in their regular seat around the table, had created an impenetrable union. They spent their formidable years growing together, shaping each other, loving one another to the fullest definition of their relations; brother and sister, fiancée, in-law, husband and wife, friends. It was a tight group. No secrets. No embarrassment.

Ethan stood over the table, grabbed the bottle of wine, and filled Maggie's glass. She took the glass and drank. Somehow,

16

without words or visible expression of any sort, she managed to thank him in a way that only he and she were aware of. His arm is her arm and he pours her wine and she drinks it down and he tastes what she tastes and they agree the first bottle was better than the second and she thanks him for being the gentleman that he is, pouring her glass before his, and all this is done not with words, but with a connection that can only be earned through years of devotion and time and love.

"Rach?" Ethan asked as he tilted the bottle over her glass.

"Please," she said. Rachel held her glass an inch or two above her antique wooden table to assist the pour.

"Winslow?"

No. The answer was always no, but Ethan always asked, with a sense of sarcasm. After topping off his own glass he took Winslow's cup to the kitchen and emptied the last of filtered water jug into it. Winslow had been sober for over nine years, an impressive statistic in its own right, but not as impressive as the fact that he also hadn't missed a single meeting during those nine years. Winslow Montgomery was committed to creating a better life for himself and for his wife, his family. He faced his sobriety with an exceptional seriousness, though he wasn't a stick in the mud, he had fun, and never once tried to stop others from having their own fun. Ethan found it admirable. To have the strength to avoid alcohol for nine years in a city as drunk as St. Louis, Missouri, the man should have a bronze statue erected in his honor. But Winslow's commitment, his promise to himself, and the ability to honor that commitment, earned him a certain level of love and respect among the people who loved him most. So, even if he had said yes, even if he desperately wanted a glass, a sip even, Ethan wasn't about to let it happen.

From the next room over, a record player produced the sweet sound of Chet Baker's trumpet. Ethan walked back to the table with his brother-in-law's glass and, being the self-proclaimed

17

Ar*tist* of the group, began to pontificate on the intricacies of Matt Damon's performance in *The Talented Mr. Ripley*, his subtle portrait of a man who the audience could so easily hate with a lesser Actor at the helm, his strength and vulnerability, playing against one another, and of course, his spot on impression of Chet's cover, "My Funny Valentine." Did they know it was Matt, not Chet, on the soundtrack? Maggie knew. She began to laugh, slowly at first, then building to an uncontrollable giggle. She'd heard Ethan's "Matt in Ripley" speech before, many times, though she wasn't laughing at him. Love was laughing. There were times in their relationship when she would sit back and look at her man. She would fall deeper in love with him for a brief, deep, moment and then, as if in celebration, she would laugh from her belly. Never too loud, never for show. Always out of love and always the same: an uncontrollable, beautiful, sexy giggle. He looked at the ring on her finger and knew how lucky he was.

Margaret Katherine Patrick. Maggie Patrick, soon to be Maggie Katherine Atkinson, laughed and laughed. Her laughter threw her to the side of the chair and the perfect muscles of her perfect bottom flexed hard to keep her from falling out of her seat. Ethan loved those muscles. He loved to wake up every morning, sometimes in the middle of the night, and find those perfect muscles relaxed, elegantly curved and sloped, buried somewhere between the sheets, her back and her legs and her feet. She liked to lie on her stomach, exposing the soft skin that clothed those perfect muscles holding her in that chair as she giggled from side to side. He looked at her and smiled. That uncontrollable giggle could center him as quickly as the flick of a switch could illuminate a dark room. He took her in, and as he took her in, his knees buckled. He was still capable of being love struck. It took all that he had to refrain from making love to her right then and there, in that moment, on his sister's kitchen table.

Rachel ate the last of the corn. She didn't ask. She didn't have to; it was her house. And being as comfortable as they were with one another it wasn't uncommon for manners to be thrown to the wayside. While Winslow cleared the table, a rare moment occurred where not one of the four was speaking. Rachel finished the corn, Winslow walked back and forth with hands full of dishes, and Ethan basked in his love for his fiancé. She kissed him and grabbed his thigh. A simple gesture of 'I love you.' He placed his hand on hers and squeezed his fingers between her fingers. 'I love you too.'

As was customary for these parties with this particular crowd, the guitar case opened and the bongos were brought to the table. Without any kids around the adults were free to play. Rachel kicked the needle from the record and Ethan took his cue to strum. His fingers danced across the strings. He *owned* the guitar and played it the way it wanted to be played, sliding his fingers across its neck with each chord. The guitar opened its mouth wide and smiled as it sang, and it sang with such pleasure, such cooperation.

Winslow, the only professional musician at the table, the paid musician, the audio engineer, set the tone on the opposite side of the dining room table. The rhythm of his drum beat swayed the women from side to side, like a tennis match was being played inside their bodies. Back and forth, the bongo and the guitar hit the little green ball, and in round, they sang, making up new words, new poems, new music. They took turns spitting out words to the never before sung song, harmonizing on the refrain. There were no egos or self-censorship in the circle, no judgment, and no pain. Sure, they would mock and make fun, but it came from a good corner of their hearts. In this circle – around this table, at night around a campfire, or in a grassy park on a sunny day, wherever they may be – their souls left their bodies, and joined hands before them. Like little, hippy children, with flowers in their long unkempt hair, their souls would groove to whatever noise their bodies could create. And it was bliss. In a world with mounting bills and ever-growing responsibilities, where wars were fought daily and security was only a job title, where politicians spent their days exploiting society's fears for their own financial gains, and in a world where schools deemed art expendable, these four thirty-something's found a way to make their own peace within it all.

They danced. They sang. Creation and laughter. Hearts were light.

NOVEMBER 20

Fire was coursing through his blood stream. It wasn't bringing warmth or excitement, rather, the fire was aching, searching for a cure and burning everything in its path. The fire was wild, uncontrollable, and his blue veins were quickly turning to dark ash. He needed her. She was the drug and he was addicted. It burnt to walk, blink, talk, to shift in his chair; anything that required motion was painful. It was severe third degree burns for his innards. Small, calculated movements were all he could tolerate, and so he sat motionless. The eyes across the table were the only thing that could hold his slumping body erect. The eyes, her eyes, held the end of a string that connected all of his bones together. Had her attention been diverted he would've collapsed to the floor like a marionette without a master. When she relaxed and sat back into her chair, he was pulled across the table, closer to her. He craved her. Not for who she was but for what she could provide. She embodied the illusion – the illusion that he packaged and sold to himself – that he was okay, that he could be okay. Her red hair was alive! It was living and it was proof that he too could move on to something new and strange and far better than what he'd just let go. With her, with those eyes and that red hair, he felt his heart could race again with another. This woman, sitting across from him in this rank and dirty Southside bar, had lifted his spirits, had shown him a different side of life and a better way to live it.

But she didn't see him, she couldn't. Sure, those eyes, those magnetic gray eyes, buried their hooks into his, but she didn't *see* him. She didn't *know* him. She looked through him only to see what it was he could do for her, which at this point, judging by his haggard appearance, his overgrown facial hair, his general neglect of personal hygiene, was nothing. He was a warm body, just flesh to rub up against, nothing more. And maybe that's all he'd ever been. Meat. Yet, given the circumstances, somehow, that was more than enough for Ethan, it was everything. He stared through her too. He didn't know her. He tried to, but only to an extent that could be of service to him.

When they met, he was wounded, and she volunteered to be his healer, to heal him in her own way, with *her* touch. Staring at him, across the tiny table in the bar where they first met, she knew she'd failed. For months she'd hoped he would amount to more than the others, more than just a memory, but now she knew he was not, nor would he ever be. Why, she asked herself, do I keep attracting the wrong man. Like a terrible poker player, she put all her chips in the pot, waiting for one last miracle card, knowing full well she was drawing dead. But she couldn't help it. Deep down, she knew it wouldn't work, that it never had a chance from the start, not with all he was going through, but she loved him, she thought so anyway, and being around him made her feel needed. And that was more than any of the others had ever done.

With his right hand, Ethan reached out blindly until he found his whiskey and melted ice. His left arm was helping the wall, and the string in her eye, hold the weight of his heavy head.

"You look ravishing," he said between sips before slowly putting his whiskey glass back on the table.

She said nothing, but she smiled and tucked a piece of her thick red hair behind her ear and wondered if he had followed her to the bar or if it was just a coincidence, as he'd claimed.

Thump...Thump...Thump. The beat from the DJ booth shook the walls and the floor. Whiskey ripples formed in his glass. He poured the rest of his drink down his throat, a Band-Aid for a wound that needed stitches.

"Let's get out of here, huh?" he said, shaking his glass to be sure it was empty. "What do you say? Go back to your place?" It was more of an instruction than a question. He stood up from the table and extended his hand, waiting for her to take it and walk out with him.

"How'd you know I'd be here?" she asked, looking up at him and smiling.

"I didn't."

"I thought you ran away. Disappeared or something."

"I'm right here," he said, waving his arm at her, calling for her to stand up.

Ethan had no idea what was next. Neither did she. But they left anyway, hand in hand, and walked into their last moments together.

JULY 16

"It's time to do it, babe," Ethan said sitting down on the edge of the mattress. "Gotta face the day. Here, sit up. Careful, it's hot." He held a coffee mug, embroidered with the letter 'M' – a gift he'd given her last Christmas (his mug was adorned with the corresponding 'E') – up to her mouth. The bean's aroma in the steam moved her nostrils from side to side, like Samantha in Bewitched, except, the only spell cast was the one that pulled her out of a dream and into the morning.

Maggie groaned something indistinguishable in reply, sat up on one elbow, and took a cautious sip. As her eyes became accustom to the daylight, her fiancée's broad shoulders, and strong back muscles, came into focus. She loved him. She loved waking this way, with coffee and gentle kisses along her neck and cheek, and it happened almost every day since they'd decided to move in together. Ethan had a habit of waking with the sunrise and he was always quiet enough not to wake her with his morning routine, a routine which always ended with coffee in bed. It was in these early morning moments, when he stood in front of their massive bedroom window, drapes pulled back so he could take in the full view of Tower Grove Park below, that she relished in the immense amount of love she had for him. Each morning confirmed the strength of what they'd created. Not that she ever had doubts, there were rarely doubts, but the day was long and full of moments where their connection could seem weak or vague, and to start each morning with such positive affirmation was a blessing she fully cherished.

Maggie put the mug on the nightstand and adjusted her body to sneak a better view of him. She could see the contour of his butt through his underwear and it tickled her. It was a miracle, she thought, that after nine years they were still so attracted to each other. With a simple look he could make her wet. She hoped he would turn from the window and throw that very look over his broad strong shoulder. Perhaps, if he caught her staring at him, if he turned and saw her face and read her mind, maybe then he would walk slowly from the window, over to the bed and, without words, gently force her to lie back. He would take all of her ass in his hands and slide the tips of his fingers beneath the elastic band of her underwear and gently pull them past her lips and her thighs and her knees, feet, toes...

"Better get moving, girl. Don't wanna be late." Ethan turned and looked at her. It wasn't *the* look. "I already let you sleep in a little this morning."

Maggie abruptly buried her face in the duvet, trying to avoid the sunlight, the day, her work, wanting to go back to her dream.

"It's not fair," she said from beneath the covers. "I want summers off too."

If she gets summers off, they don't pay rent. Or if they pay rent then they buy used instead of leasing new. They had a nice life, a nice lifestyle even, but it depended on a dual-family income.

Ethan pulled a pair of sweatpants over his underwear. A hooded sweatshirt covered his bare chest and back. The foot of the bed sank as he sat. It wasn't going to happen, the simple look, not this morning, anyway. Maggie tossed the covers off of her body and wrestled momentarily with the sheets, which were tangled around her legs. She could feel him sneak a peek at her. It felt nice to be noticed, but it was a distant consolation prize. She'd make him pay. She'd make him think of her, masturbate even. She pulled her underwear off and left them by the side of the bed. Then, like a runway model, she took long, subtle, catwalk strides past Ethan on her way to the bathroom. She could feel her own curves, her own lines at the tops of her legs, and they flowed and swayed rhythmically, like water in a pool, as she stomped away. She slammed the bathroom door. A happy, grumpy slam. Good morning.

AUGUST 15

His shoelaces were untied and tucked into the insole. That's how he liked to find them each morning. He would always untie them when he finished running, and carefully tuck the laces beneath the tongue so they wouldn't dangle from the shoe rack. He valued the shoes too much to ruin the heel by sliding them on and off every day. If the heel was crushed, the support would be flimsy, it wouldn't fit around the ankle as it was designed, and he would be forced to buy new shoes before the traction was fully worn down. With just several extra seconds of effort, the shoe would last. Ethan was a bit OCD in this habit but he valued his running shoes, they were part of the morning routine, they represented his run therapy mantra: take care of your feet, take care of your body, take care of your mind. Running exercised his thoughts and kept him free, mentally, to control his psyche.

Ethan learned this from his father, John Atkinson. John would keep a similar routine with his footwear, though his other, more damaging idiosyncrasies, carried over to many additional aspects of Ethan and Rachel's lives. After breakfast, enforcing his own morning routine, the milk cartons had to face a specific direction when being placed back into the refrigerator. That way, when John, or Rachel or Ethan went to pour, there would be no need to rotate the carton. It was only a matter of *efficiency*. Efficiency was to blame for many things; for the books being placed in alphabetical order (by author and then by title if multiple books were owned by the same author), for extra trash bags being placed at the bottom of the trash can, and for the car, when gas was running low, to be filled up at night, instead of the following morning. Simple enough, and much of it made sense.

But *efficiency* was also the reason Ethan had a scar on his jaw, to the left of his chin. If, for instance, the laundry was not placed in the drawer correctly (socks on the left, underwear on the right, just as mother had done), or the dishes dried improperly (glasses were to be placed down on a towel over night and then hand dried the following morning to remove spots, just as mother had done), John would act out physically, usually at the expense of his children; sometimes with a spoon (a quick flick to the wrist would remove elbows from a table), but usually with the back of his hand.

The scar on Ethan's jaw appeared, and permanently remained, several days after the chunky purple scab had healed. John Atkinson was working in his garage. To his credit, he'd decided to spend some quality time with his kids, organizing the tools in their basement. Maybe they'd learn a thing or two, he figured. But being children, they quickly grew disinterested and started giggling at one another, poking, the beginnings of roughhousing. Ethan and Rachel expanded their game into a sword fight, using a crescent wrench and screwdriver, respectively. John

Atkinson still wore his wedding ring – antique style with a diamond in its center, almost like a class ring – and when he struck Ethan's face with the back of his left hand, the diamond took a good sized dollop of flesh along with it as it crossed his jaw.

Still, there was something to efficiency. Apples don't fall far, and while Ethan vowed to never strike his future children, he did manage to inherit a few efficient traits.

Ethan opened the bathroom door and kissed his fiancée. She kissed back, looking into his eyes. They made a point to connect as often as possible, and locking eyes during a kiss good bye was a standard. Ethan left the apartment, as per routine, to run. To run away from his thoughts, to run through his thoughts.

Tower Grove South, the roughly fifteen square block neighborhood just south of the park, the South Side, as it's affectionately known by Ethan and its other inhabitants, had been his home since his second year at St. Louis University, and the old brick duplex was home since his junior year, when he met Maggie. He grew to love the area, despite its high crime rate and rundown buildings, largely because of the time he spent running through the park. The huge oak trees stood tall and proud with a century's worth of stories to tell. The flowering dogwoods would bloom an innocent white or pink flower reminding him that all was not lost in the world. And weekends brought droves of people to the park's fields, new people, new faces, new names. Each time he ran through the park his eyes would be struck with amusement at some new sight he had yet to take in. Ethan ran daily, except Saturday, and whittled the three mile trip around the park into a thirty minute scenic workout.

That was before his sister had moved into the Shaw neighborhood, north of the park, the North Side. His sister brought his brother-in-law, Winslow Montgomery. Winslow wanted to "get in shape," and that constituted a change in the routine. Ethan loved Rachel, and therefore loved Winslow, but the private therapy run where thoughts were to be worked out alone had suddenly become a group session.

The route was always the same: cross Arsenal to enter the park, take the outer bike path down to Central Cross drive, where Ethan would wait a number of minutes for Winslow to show (he was habitually late), and from there they would run the perimeter of the park. When the run was finished, they'd hug in a brief manly fashion, and break off to their respective homes. They ran like this every day, except Saturday, for years, and after the first several months, Ethan's eyes began to find new things again. Eventually, he accepted the change in his routine, something his father never learned to do. The apple grew its own roots and aimed to stand tall on its own.

In the center of the park, where Central Cross drive formed a turnabout, there was a massive, full length, statue of William Shakespeare, a gift to the park from Henry Shaw, Shaw being the parks founder and designer. The statue was the agreed upon meeting point for Ethan and Winslow, since Winslow came from the North Side, and Ethan's duplex bordered the south side of the park. It was a logical centralized location. Even though he knew he was on time, and figured Winslow would be somewhere between four and twelve minutes late, Ethan checked his watch. He decided to look around, to amuse himself until his brother-in-law showed.

Just a stone's throw from the Bill Shakespeare statue, there were fenced-in grass tennis courts. Ethan never played tennis, maybe once or twice whenever it was required in high school gym class, but he loved the horticulture within Tower Grove Park, and grass that could survive the trampling of a tennis match deserved a closer look. Plus, thanks to Winslow, he had time to kill.

The chain link fence surrounding the courts was cold when he placed his fingers through its diamond shaped slots. He put both hands and his forearms against the metal; it was a welcomed shock to his skin. He could feel an acorn crush beneath his shoe; the massive oaks were shedding early. The air was crisp but the dogs playing in the park, the ones he was now watching, didn't seem to mind. They opened their coats to embrace the morning air while their owners stood shoulder to shoulder in fleece or North Face jackets, admiring what fine animals they had raised. He'd given up on the grass. The dogs were in motion and it was far more interesting.

Through the fence holes he watched one particular mutt working for attention from his peers. Once it had drummed up enough interest from the others, he began to lead them in large circles. The mutt was in full stride, four or five lengths ahead of the pack, turning his head every so often to make sure they were still following. He was faster than the rest. It was a Labrador mix, Ethan guessed, wandering if the dog lacked attention in the home. That would explain his dire need for acceptance amongst his peers. Or was dog psychology different from human psychology? Ethan had never owned a dog. He'd always wanted one, but his grandmother claimed she had allergies, so it never happened. And at this point, he thought, it was too late. Maggie was his companion and she supplied all the emotional gratification he could desire. The lead mutt came barreling down on the proud owners, brushing past the backs of their knees at full speed. The other dogs followed, nearly taking the group of owners to the ground. The humans all laughed. Proud, proud parents they all were.

The lab-mix-mutt stopped on a dime behind a wooden bench, kicking grass and dirt in the air. His face was on the ground between his front paws, his ass in the air, tail wagging. He was in a faceoff with the other dogs, they had him cornered and he loved it! But there was an innocent victim caught in the crossfire. A girl, a woman, was sitting in the bench holding a book and watching the same game of Chase. The pack would have to go through her to get to the mutt. The woman laughed. She was nervous but it was fun. Ethan moved a few chain links over to recalibrate his view. She was cute, pretty even, but not in the traditional sense. He watched her as she carefully set her book to the side and threw her red hair back in a ponytail, readying herself for battle. No one made a move. After several moments the mutt grew impatient and barked, startling the not-traditionally-attractive-girl. She was wrapped up in the excitement and laughed out loud. There was *something* about her, Ethan thought. There was something intriguing below her surface.

He was still engrossed with the bench-woman long after the dogs had gone about running and playing elsewhere. That thing about her, that *something,* he decided, was sadness. A deep seeded sadness, one that was not easily remedied: father issues, maybe even a rape. This sadness quality was not at all uncommon among the artistic women of the Tower Grove neighborhoods. Perhaps it was a step-father. Maybe that's why she'd decided to dye her hair that awful shade of red. That's why she read books in parks. What book was it? Probably *Jane Eyre* or maybe *The Unbearable Lightness of Being*. It was definitely something of the classics. She wore thick stockings beneath her boots and a gently-used skirt that appeared to have seen more years than she had lived. That sort of style would settle for nothing less than the classics. She was a hipster. Ethan wasn't sure what that term, *hipster,* meant exactly but he had heard his sister use it whenever groups of people, people who dressed similarly to this bench-woman, would walk into The Royale, their neighborhood bar. Ethan owned several vintage sweaters that Maggie had purchased for him over the years, and he smoked pot too. Therefore, he surmised, he too could maybe be a hipster. Surely he's read that book, whatever it was. Bukowski? They could be friends if he wanted. If he chose. If he walked over to her, sat on the bench next to her, and asked for

32

her opinion on that progressive novel, whatever the hell it was. Maggie would love her too. Maggie had seen girls like this in the neighborhood and always commented on them. "I love that purse... I'd kill to chop my hair off like that... Don't they have jobs?" Yes, Maggie would love her too. Maggie. Maggie. She too would find her instantly attractive. She too would want to get to the bottom of that deep seeded sadness, the root of the intrigue. The bench-woman picked up her book, found her dog-eared page and settled back into the novel.

The fence had barely warmed in the spots where Ethan hung his arms when a hand slapped his shoulder. The hand hit him far too hard to belong to a stranger.

"You know, you hang around a playground without a kid and you're a pervert," Winslow said. "You watch a bunch of dogs in a park, and you don't bring a dog, no one seems to think twice." He had a point. It suddenly did feel quite creepy, what he was doing. "Hey, let's get rollin'. I gotta get home before your sister breaks my balls for not cleaning the hairs off the bathroom sink," he said, now squeezing Ethan's shoulder. "You really should get a dog, man."

They ran in silence, heel giving way to toe, one foot in front of the other, for thirty consecutive minutes, keeping pace with each other, never pushing, always maintaining. It was rare for men to relate to one another without some form of competition, but these two were an exception. For three years they ran like this, bonding through proximity and silence, becoming more and more like the brothers the law said they were.

They broke off Northwest drive after the Foreman's Residence and finished their run on the bike trail. They hugged, one armed, like men, and made plans for dinner later in the week. Winslow went north on Central Cross drive. Ethan went south.

JUNE 28
&
SEPTEMBER 2

Thin noodles were swimming vigorously with nowhere to go as the water boiled and bubbled, threatening to dive over the edge of the pot. Ethan lowered the flame and the waters calmed. Combining the salt and pepper, oil, vinegar, red wine, garlic, and balsamic ingredients together in a mason jar, he screwed the lid on tight, and shook them until they were one. The needle dropped on the outer edge of the record. The oven timer sang. Ethan took the towel draped over his shoulder and wiped his brow. He was juggling, but he was in control. He was perspiring, but not from the pressure, from the rush. Like a veteran athlete in the final moments of the big game, he knew the play and he executed it to perfection. He popped open the oven with his left hand and removed the baguette with is right. A chef in his kitchen, flowing to his own rhythm. He grated the provolone over the French bread and turned, a twirl, a pivot, back to the oven where the cheese and the garlic and the butter and the bread become one. It was a dance! Set the table. Waltz! Pour the dressing. Tango! Add the ground sausage to the sauce, mushrooms and onions, oregano. Cha-cha! Hustle! Jitter-bug!

The front door of the duplex opened letting some of the hot air out of the apartment. Maggie dropped her purse at the door and kicked off her heels, leaving a trail of clothes and accessories on her way to the kitchen.

"Smells good," she said.

She opened the refrigerator, ducked her head in, and came out with the half empty bottle of pinot from the night before. She partially filled a glass and swallowed it down like a shot before pouring another, a full glass this time, the "relax and unwind" glass.

Ethan found a moment between preparations to prop himself on the counter top and observe her actions. She was a whirlwind of stress and energy, but he was well aware and got out of her way. He couldn't help but smile at the furry she could work herself into. A day at the office, in her tight pantsuit, running in circles, commanding respect from clients and fellow employees alike, could wind her so tight. She was good at her job and he knew it. It was even attractive to a certain extent. But unlike Ethan, Maggie never wanted to talk about work. She left the job at the office. For a brief moment in their relationship this had bothered him. Why wouldn't she want to open up and share her day? If she's not talking with him then surely there was some other man in her office, some taller, better looking man she must be relating to, and he probably had a huge bank account and a huge... His mind had a tendency to spiral out of control if he allowed such things.

Ethan's fears were dispelled with one blow out fight. The word *Trust* was defined and thrown about repeatedly until eventually he understood, with mild embarrassment, that it was his own insecurities that needed the attention.

So, Maggie would come home, bottle her stress, un-bottle some wine, and in fifteen minutes she'd be fine. And Ethan learned to accept this about her. Stand aside, let the wine do its thing, and in a short time, he'd find the woman he loved.

"You need one?" She asked.

"I'm drinking red."

Ethan strained the pasta in the sink and the steam filled his face. He could feel his pores opening. Maggie took the towel from his shoulder and padded him down, drying him off before kissing him 'hello.'

"I'm gonna change," Maggie said, kissing him again. "Let's eat on the balcony. The oven makes it so damn hot in here. Oh, and don't mix the sauce and the noodles. Just… can you just put it a bowl on the side." She kissed him once more and left the kitchen, picking her high heels up off of the floor on her way out.

Two plates were made, one with a bowl of meat sauce on the side. He walked past the spinning record, and headed toward the French double doors that opened to the balcony. Holding both plates, Ethan changed course and ducked his head into the bedroom. There was something he wanted to tell her, something small, a detail about his day, or some upcoming event, nothing really. But the moment he saw her, whatever it was had escaped his mind. Standing there in the doorway, staring at Maggie, he found a moment he wanted to savor.

He watched as she pulled the pencil skirt off of her legs and down to her toes. She wore a black thong, maybe lace; he didn't care, the details were in her skin. Maggie was still wound tight and it stifled her awareness. She couldn't feel his eyes or his presence in the room. He was a voyeur in his own home. Maggie pulled a pair of old nursing scrubs from her dresser drawer and stepped into them. She was so undeniably sexy, to move in this way, without a hint of awkwardness or loss of balance. She was fluid, with grace and elegance in each movement, and it was a thing of beauty. Sure, he thought to himself, it was one thing to move like this when the subject is aware of the watchful eye, but to flow like water, to possess such presence, even in the most private of moments, was certainly a unique attribute.

He loved those scrubs, the ones she'd just slid on, from the first time he'd seen her in them, back in college. He gave in and decided to stay in her dorm that night, not that it had taken much convincing on her part. Blue hospital scrubs, baggy and unbecoming, but with the shape of her butt beneath the drawstring waist, they drove Ethan mad with desire. She wore them almost every night. Her house pants, as he commonly referred to them, and he felt lucky to know her.

From time to time, there were moments that happened in life that could take Ethan's breath away, a flower in bloom, the innocent laughter from one of his students, the sound of the wind moving through trees in the park across the street. These moments were rare; maybe once or twice per week, but only if he remained open could he find them. Watching Maggie transform from business woman to fiancée was one such moment. Ethan leaned on the door casing and let the joists within the walls absorb his weight. His eyes settled on her like a ship dropping anchor. And as she removed her blouse, and replaced it with her favorite Guns N' Roses t-shirt, he succumbed to a daydream, a memory. A sense of déjà vu washed over him as Maggie stood atop their bed on her tippy toes, her hair now short, barely tucked behind her tiny ears. She was wearing the scrubs and the t-shirt, and her arms were stretched out wide across a painted and framed canvas. She tugged at the bottom corner and stood back a few steps on the mattress to take a look.

37

"What do you think? Even?" she said.

When she turned to face him her eyes were glowing. A strand of brown hair found its way out from behind her ear. She tucked it back into place and smiled the sweetest, softest smile that had ever been smiled.

"It's even, right?" Maggie hopped to the foot of the bed and sat. "This is our home. We have a home!" she said, still glowing. Then she spread her arms and fell back into the mattress. She rolled her eyes back to look at the painting she'd just hung above her head. "Are you okay with it there? I like it."

The painting, one Maggie had completed in her last year of college, was a graduation present she had given herself, and she hung it on the wall like a diploma, marking her accomplishment. It was also the final project in her ART 320 PAINTING II class. The painting was red from corner to corner. Abstract. Several darker shades of the same color slashed their way toward the middle and a thin black stroke pulled attention to the center of the canvas. It was her pride, something that show her potential, the *what might've been* of her Artistic Dreams.

She rolled off the bed and walked toward the massive window that overlooked Tower Grove Park. "We have a home, baby. I love you."

•

Ethan watched her disappear out of the window. He scanned the room. It was different now, it was empty. There were sheets on the bed, but it was unmade, with its covers kicked to the floor. The room was suddenly void of any color. Her dresser, gone. Candles, gone. Feminine touch, gone. And the painting, the vibrant red painting Maggie had spent so much time creating, was no longer hanging above the headboard. The hole, where the nail

38

pierced the wall to hold the frame, was the only thing that remained as proof of her existence.

Ethan's hands were empty too, the plates of pasta, gone, cooked for another day in another life. He pulled himself from the doorframe and took heavy steps toward the bed. Sitting at the foot, looking back at the empty, unkempt sheets, his hand floated over a vacant spot among the mess of bedding. There was wrath in his fists as he tore the elastic edge of sheet from the corners of the bed, exposing the bare mattress. Ethan pushed the tips of his fingers into the cushion, reaching, or digging, for something. Beneath his hands, imprinted into the fabric of the mattress, was the thin outline of a stain. A blood stain, cleaned and dried, small, but noticeable.

SEPTEMBER 12

"Those kids need you. Stop talking out of your ass," Rachel said as she set three plates on the center of the table next to a small pile of silverware, three forks, three steak knives. She'd grabbed four initially, still out of habit, but she managed to return the extra to the drawer unnoticed. "They should be your refuge right now," she said. "You like your job. Fuck, Eth, you love your job."

Ethan was silent.

She pulled a chair out from beneath the dining room table and sat next to her brother. "Listen, I have no idea how hard this is for you. But I do know you've got family. I know those kids are like family." She waited for a reply, waited for him to stop gazing out the window and connect with her. "Ethan. Are you listening to me?"

"Yes," he said, without blinking an eye.

"Why the hell am I explaining all this to you? You know why you teach." She paused for a moment, resting her chin on her fist, trying to think of what perfect words she could say. The truth of it was Ethan was pulling her down. She wanted to be happy but couldn't, not with her brother looking so miserable.

"You know you mean more to them than their own damn parents," she continued, one last ditch effort. "You wanna piss on my weekend because your personal life is taking a dip? That's fine, I'm your sister, I'm here for that. But, those kids, they need to feel good about life. About themselves. And like it or not, Eth, your energy is contagious. It's shitty and contagious. They pick up on it. I pick up on it. Fuck, mother nature is picking up on it." Rachel made a gesture toward her back patio where Winslow was standing alongside the barbeque grill, tongs in one hand, and an umbrella in the other, sheltering himself from the heavy clouds rolling over his head.

Rachel got up from the table and walked back into the kitchen, pulled a glass from the cabinet, and filled it with tap water.

"*Taking a dip*?" Ethan said.

"What?"

"My personal life is *taking a dip*?"

"It's not what I meant," she said, trying to recover. "I just don't wanna see you like this. You're a happy person. We're a happy family."

Rachel looked out the window above her kitchen sink at her husband. She waved at him and he made one of his many goofy faces back at her, he continued to work the meat over the hot coals. A dichotomy of emotions left Rachel speechless. Inside, she wanted to support and rescue her brother from this sudden onset of depression. Outside, she wanted to dance and celebrate with the love of her life in the rain. Ethan's pain directly conflicted with Rachel's happiness, leaving her unfulfilled. Rachel wanted nothing more than to open up and share the good news with her brother, but the timing was wrong. She knew that what she had to say would only make things worse.

Rachel turned back to her brother. "I'm sorry. I didn't mean to come down on you." She walked back to Ethan, bent herself over the back of his chair, and wrapped her arms around her brother. They were cheek to cheek. "I'm being insensitive. I miss her too." She could feel his eyes blinking rapidly as he fought off tears.

"It's more than that," he said gripping his sister's forearms.

"I know."

They were blood. And it ran deep.

Brother, sister, family, friend; these words, even when expressed to their fullest, could not justifiably describe their relationship. Blood, though, blood carried something extra, something thicker, something that could not easily wash away over time.

Rachel pulled away, breaking the embrace, but Ethan continued to blink, harder now, his eyelashes mopping up the mess in the corners of his eyes. Rachel walked toward the hall desk, where she and Winslow kept piles of junk mail and other unpaid bills, and pretended to sort through and organize them. All the while, her mind was stuck on the large, legal envelope resting on the corner of the desk, separate from the rest of the pile. Finally, when the urge was too strong to suppress, she lifted the envelope and held it in her hands, debating her next move.

With one hand holding a tray of food and the other gripping both the tongs, and the umbrella, Winslow used his elbow to open the sliding glass door. He shook off the puddle of rain water that had gathered on his shoulders and boots before entering the house. Steam, and the smell of freshly grilled barbeque pork steaks, escaped from beneath the tin foil covering the plate in his hand. "A black man cookin' in the rain for you two. Your grandparents would be so proud," Winslow said, setting the tray down beside the plates and silverware. "Hey?" he said noticing the envelope in her hands. "Now?"

Rachel turned to her husband and smiled softly. "Yes. Now," she said.

Rachel sat down in the chair beside her brother and pulled all of his attention onto her. "I know it's not the right time. I know. But I can't keep anything from you." They were face to face, and Ethan could see that water was building in her eyes. "Open it," she said, presenting the envelope to Ethan. He was confused and nervous but he smiled for the first time. The envelope was not sealed and its flap was tucked into its body. Inside, there were several pieces of paper. As he removed the paper from the envelope, his smile quickly faded into tightened, straight lips. Ethan stared at the paper, unsure of what to say, and even more unsure of what to feel.

"I'm at five weeks."

"We found out Friday," said Winslow.

Ethan tucked the ultrasound photos back into the envelope and labored through an artificial smile, showing the whites of his teeth. He walked to them, forcing his joints to open and close with each heavy step, and shook his brother-in-law's hand. He took another heavy step and engulfed Rachel in his arms. They all tried in vain to stifle their emotions, the clash of joy and regret, excitement and bitterness, pulling on each of them.

When he finally let go of his sister, Ethan opened the sliding glass door and walked out into the rain. He sat on the top stair of their deck and the water quickly soaked his hair and shoulders. He refused to blink now. Staring into a wall of rain drops, he questioned why everything, this avalanche of shit, was happening to him. Why now? Why were the last few weeks so cruel?

Rachel slipped out the door and sat beside him, holding the umbrella over both their heads, and together they sat quietly, each knowing what the other was thinking, each knowing there was nothing that could be said to make the situation right. But the pounding of the raindrops on the umbrella overhead provided a comforting rhythm, a soothing sound that echoed the mood.

SEPTEMBER 1

The strong fragrance of lemon-infused cleaning product tickled the hairs on the inside of Ethan's nose. He squeezed the trigger on the plastic bottle several times and pulled a wad of paper towels across the dusty chalkboard. The result was night and day. A shinny dark green board was uncovered, ready to be released on the new school year. He removed several long pieces chalk from a cardboard box and placed them in pairs on the left, middle, and right sides of the grooved chalk container jutting out from the wall. They would be broken or lost within weeks but the start of the year always brought hope, and that hope bred organization; cleanliness is, after all, next to godliness. Ethan had started each new school year in this manner, going back to his first days in kindergarten. Pencils neatly sharpened and placed into their pencil box, three ring binders loaded with fresh paper, books covered with homemade grocery bag covers (plain side facing up so designs and doodles could be created throughout the year). The good feeling that the "First Day of School" brought had usually dissipated by the end of the first week, but it was exciting nonetheless, and made for a special energy in the classroom. As he lay out the chalk pieces in a neat and orderly fashion and set a fresh, clean eraser next to them, he sensed a tinge, an imprint of his father seeping though. Organization and efficiency. Ethan felt a subconscious itch near the scar on his jaw. Reaching up with the bottom of his palm, he scratched it.

Ethan hung an inspirational poster on the wall – COURAGE, penguins diving from an iceberg – and unloaded the remaining contents of the cardboard box: Rubik's cube, rubber-band ball, Far Sides calendar, snack box full of Graham crackers. When he sat back in his creaky old chair, he noticed a void, a vacant spot on his desk where Maggie should have been staring back at him through a picture frame. When he packed his things earlier in the day he deliberately left that frame at home in a box on the floor of the hall closet. He rearranged the things on his desk to try and hide the empty spot – moved the calendar, took a notepad from the drawer and placed it beside the Far Sides calendar – but in the end, nothing felt right. Nothing but the frame, with her inside, would make him feel right. She was still there, in the same vacant spot, and he could feel her existence. He could still hear her voice in a quiet room.

The chair creaked and Ethan looked up at the empty desks, ready to meet their young faces, but the room was empty, he was alone. Ethan pulled at the hairs on the back of his head, wondering what the year would be like without her, if she would come back like he'd told himself time and time again she would. *Next year, maybe, with time.* Truth be told, he didn't even want her back. She'd betrayed him. But now, without her, there would be no one to come home to after work, no inside jokes, no romantic baths, no one to make pasta for or share a morning coffee with, no partner to listen to the stories about his day, and listen to him repeat all of the crazy things the students had said. All that she left was a pillow, a pillow without a heartbeat. No Maggie. His breath was shallow as his eyes drifted over the vacant spot on the desk and into the sea of empty chairs. She still filled the room. She filled every empty thought and empty space in Ethan's life. Her presence was inescapable.

Ethan heard a knock, and from the corner of his eye he saw a towering figure in the doorway. It was Principal Fenske, leaning the top half of her large body in the classroom as she knocked on the door. It was polite bullshit, part of her game, just the thing Ethan hated about Fenske. Fenske liked to pretend everyone was equal, but she'd be pretending from her soapbox as she looked down upon all the little people. At five foot eleven, and always wearing two inch heels for added effect, she didn't even need the soapbox; she looked down on almost everyone that worked for her. Everyone but Ethan, who, at six foot one, looked her dead in the eye. That didn't stop her from playing mind games. Fenske had charm, she could wink and smile her way through anything, and on most people, parents especially, it worked. But it made Ethan sick. Fenske was a master manipulator, and yet, she was the principal, his boss, and she needed zero permission to enter Ethan's classroom. Moreover, she wasn't asking for any. The door was propped fully open and she walked right through, only two or three steps, just to prove she could, before Ethan could even think to invite her in.

"How was your summer?" She said with an annoying chirpiness to her voice. Phony.

Despite her bullshit, Fenske had asked a question that, for Ethan, wasn't easy to sum up with a brief, friendly answer, at least not honestly. He paused and thought for what felt like an awkward amount of time before giving any sort of response. He ran every

47

moment of the past three months through his mind and, finally, he forced a smile.

"Good! You ready for another group of these guys?" Fenske said gesturing toward the rows of empty seats.

"Looking forward to it," Ethan said.

"We're going to follow curriculum this year, right?" Fenske said, raising one eyebrow in warning. "We're going to work with the whole team?"

We? Who the fuck is *'we'*, Ethan thought. He was pulling the hair at the base of his skull a bit harder now, and he forced another smile in reply, this time a little wider.

Fenkse was referring to his track record, his reluctance to partner with fellow *team* members regarding the IEP's. Specifically, last year, when he strayed from the IEP curriculum to help a student learn at a more comfortable pace. It didn't go over well with the team, despite the fact that the child was happy, and showed better results.

IEP's, Individualized Education Programs, were the government mandated, nationwide education standard for students with special needs. The United States government created a law to provide service to children with disabilities, and to fully abide by the law's regulations, the IEP's were developed and monitored by the IEP Team. The *team* consisted of the child, his or her parents, the child's primary teacher, a qualified representative of the school district, the school psychologist, and, if the parents wanted, the child's personal psychologist. An army was built to march in and monitor Ethan's progress as a teacher, and while he adored the concept of IEP's, the acronym itself made him cringe. The thought of the *Team* coming in and shedding their intelligence, or more accurately, their opinion, on his life's work, made his insides churn. He felt the key word in IEP, *Individualized*, was lost, swallowed up by this group. And in his experience, more often than not, the army scared his students. Inevitably, it became a group of adults – adults without the disability – discussing what was best for the person with the disability, and they did this without ever asking the opinion of the one person that mattered, the person with the disability.

Ethan preferred a one on one approach: One on one with the child. One on one with the parents to explain techniques and mark progress. One on one with his boss for updates. The whole process had caused him much anxiety over the years. He felt there was a better method, and so he made it known to Fenske. But Fenske was an administrator, and administrators dealt with paperwork, not children, so his plan was rejected. Ethan fought back in small battles, utilizing his own method. He would encourage the students to open up to him, to trust him. He made private calls to parents. He went the extra mile, and it paid off. Ethan made stronger bonds with the students, and their development exceeded the national average for specially educated students. Until Fenske caught on. A parent thanked *her* for *his* extra effort midway through the last school year, and while she appreciated his passion, it was made clear to him that deviating from standard IEP practices would not be tolerated.

"Yes, of course," he said. "I'm happy to keep everyone involved this year." Ethan was sure he'd created a bald spot on the back of his head from all the hair pulling.

"Good," she said with another bullshit smile.

She left his room and it was quiet again. He felt reprimanded before the first bell had even rung. Ethan threw himself forward and the chair creaked loudly. He stood and walked to the door, lifted the door stand with his foot and let it slam behind him. It was his classroom, damn it.

Before the sound of the door slamming could clear the air, it had opened again. Unlike Fenske, Russ Winkler, the 8th graders homeroom teacher, walked in like he owned the place. And, in a sense, he did. Russ was the longest tenured teacher at Park View

Elementary, and had held his position for thirty-three years. Russ was not phony. Russ Winkler was genuine. Annoying, but genuine.

"Hey, kiddo. How you doin? Room looks great," Russ said, taking in the surroundings, comparing Ethan's classroom style to his own. "New poster, I like that. What is that? Penguins? I like it. You gotta keep the room fresh, don't ya?"

"I try," said Ethan as he stopped, turned, and sat on the corner of his desk. There was something about Russ that made Ethan feel like he had to give him his full attention, respecting elders and whatnot. As a result, Ethan was sure never to keep his back turned toward Russ.

"I say it every year; we gotta start strong if we expect the kids to give half a shit." Russ liked to give speeches. He also liked to keep morale high. Ethan gave him a lot of credit for maintaining enthusiasm for so many years. Ethan thought about what his sister had said about a person's mood being contagious. "Listen," Russ continued, "I was thinking of inviting a dad or two this year to play on Saturdays." Russ ran a weekly pickup game of basketball in the school gymnasium, and Ethan was one of the regulars. "What do you think? I figure it'll keep us from running short since Mike and Jimbo are both out. You hear about Jim?"

Ethan shook his head. He hadn't heard.

"Cancer. Can you believe that?"

"Jesus." Ethan was stunned. He actually couldn't believe it. Not that he was close with Jim, but he knew him, and knowing the person always makes it a little more real, a little harder to take.

Russ was shaking his head now in disbelief. "Can happen to any of us. Gotta keep yourself clean. And young, that seems to help. You're still good there. He's fighting it though. Things are looking pretty good. I talked to his wife the other day and she said he was staying strong. She's takin' good care of him."

50

Ethan tried to remember the last time he'd seen his doctor. Time to get checked? He still had another ten or fifteen years before certain tests were recommended, but you can't be too careful, right? He looked up at Russ, who had stopped talking. Ethan guessed he was questioning his own lifespan as well. Russ spoke first.

"Eh, youth is wasted on the young. Stay healthy, would ya? Enjoy it while ya still got it." Russ scratched the top of his head, searching through his thinning hair for the glory days. "Anyway, I just wanted to pop in. Happy new year, kiddo," he said waving over his shoulder as he walked out the door.

Again, the room was quiet, and still. The year had started. The first week hadn't even begun and the excitement was nearly gone. Taking one of the fresh chalk pieces, he wrote his name on the board in large, sprawling letters, attempting to recapture some of the joy and excitement that Fenske and Russ had sucked out. He put the chalk back its grove and sat down again, creaking the chair. The vacant spot on the desk stared back at him. For the first time, his personal life and his professional life were out of sync. He looked back at the door, wondering if he and Jim were sharing similar feelings. Probably not, he thought. Jim had a family.

AUGUST 16

It was relatively late, by working adult standards, and so the lights were off in the house, leaving only the blue-gray light from the television to illuminate their cozy bedroom. Rachel and Winslow were sitting up in bed, their backs supported by headboard and pillow, and their legs tucked, but fidgeting with excitement beneath the covers. From outside, the house looked asleep, but inside, there was laughter, the crippling kind of laughter that cramps the gut and turns even the mundane into hilarity, and it gripped them, forcing wide smiles full of teeth and gums. The television's black and white characters flickered across the screen without sound. The dialogue was being supplied by the smiling mouths in the bed across the room. Winslow was improvising lines for Montgomery Clift, and each new scene had Rachel's sides splitting further down her ribcage. She was laughing so hard she could hardly keep up with her own characters dialogue which, in turn, caused him to jump between characters to pick up her slack. He was Clift, he was Taylor, he was Shelly Winters, which nearly threw Rachel from the bed. It was "Mystery Science Theater 3000" but for the bedroom, and only with Turner's Classics, and ridiculous storylines were a must; the more absurd the better the comedy.

Frequently, their characters absurd storylines would bleed into real life. Once, during a creation/reenactment of "Manhattan", Winslow's Woody Allen made fierce love to his daughter, Mariel Hemmingway, played by Rachel. Their storyline had Woody checking up on his daughter while she was going to college at NYU. Of course, her mother, Diane Keaton (also voiced by Rachel) was furious when she heard the news of their affair. She threatened Woody, said he'd never make another movie in this town if he slept with and married his own daughter, but alas, she was wrong. Diane went on to fall madly in love with her ex-husband, and Woody (voiced by Winslow) carried on with both his ex-wife, and his hot, collegiate daughter. In the final scene of their revisionist tale, Mariel offers oral sex to her father in exchange for a foot massage. Rachel and Winslow happily agreed to the terms and as the credits rolled she disappeared under the covers. Life imitating art, making fun of art, enjoying life.

The telephone rang in Rachel and Winslow's bedroom. Montgomery Clift instructed Elizabeth Taylor to answer it, and being the type of high society girl who loved to take an order from a lowly shop boy, she did as she was told. Through laughter, Rachel answered.

"Hello?"

It was Maggie. Rachel's face abruptly changed upon hearing the tone in her voice. She rolled away from Winslow to her side of the bed.

"Slow down, Mag. What is it?"

53

After listening for several moments, she sat up fully and swung her feet out from beneath the sheets over the edge of the bed. Winslow's interest had peaked but he could only hear a muffled version of Maggie's voice escaping the ear piece. All he could think to do was flip on the bedside lamp. More listening. Rachel left the bed and began to pace the room. She turned off the TV to further avoid distraction. The pacing finally stopped and she leaned against the wall, staring at her husband with concern and sadness.

Rachel finally spoke up, "Fuck, hun. I don't know what to say. You need to talk to him…Why? … I know it is."

She slowly slid her body down the wall until she sat seated with her arms wrapped around her knees. "Do you want me to come over? You wanna meet? We can talk about it if you want. We can talk about options." Rachel looked at her husband shaking her head, giving up. He moved to the end of the bed and sat at the corner, drawing his own array of conclusions from the fragments of conversation. Rachel hung up the phone.

"What is it!?" Winslow asked.

"Maggie. She's pregnant."

He cocked his head and eyebrows with curiosity. Pregnancy was beautiful, Winslow thought to himself, even if it was unplanned. Not to mention this kid couldn't have had two parents who were more in love than Ethan and Maggie, and capable of starting a family, with the exception of he and Rach. So why then did the world suddenly come to a screeching halt? Why was his wife curled on the floor, red faced and quiet, after hearing she was only nine months away from becoming an aunt. Winslow looked at his wife, demanding answers. Rachel was distraught.

"She's not keeping it. She wants to have an abortion," she said.

The words stunned Winslow. He sat back on the bed, resting on his hands. It didn't make sense, they were in love, they

54

had a home, they had good jobs. To Winslow, there could be no conceivable reason to do such a thing, to keep this child from having a wonderful, loving life.

"What did Ethan say?"

Rachel shook her head and tears quickly formed in her eyes, not quite falling to her face, "He doesn't know. She begged me not to tell him." Rachel paused, hoping her husband would talk her out of agreeing to the ludicrous terms. "I said 'okay.' We can't tell him."

Winslow picked his bride up off of the floor and held her, saying nothing, only trying to comfort her, and assure her that things would be okay. But Rachel knew the worst was still on its way.

Secrets did not exist between Rachel and her brother. She feared for him. She knew the day would come when he would know, and he would not take it lightly. Ethan felt things to the bone, to the marrow. He wanted the most out of life, highs and lows, and this subject, his own child, would not be easily brushed under the rug. She felt the urge to protect him, to tell him, to comfort him, to be the parent she'd always been to her baby brother.

JULY 3

Ethan pulled the U-shaped handle on the coffee table to open the drawer. The table was made of wood, old wood, wood that had seen many years, or at least was designed to look like it had. The handles on the drawers were like miniature door knockers, sans the lion's face. Ethan found the table late one night on Vandeventer Avenue. He was on a drunk walk back from Humphries Tavern, when he saw it sitting in the middle of the sidewalk, bathing in light from the streetlamp above. It looked like a gift from god, a sign, and he swore the old wooden table called to him, "Take me to your home, Ethan Atkinson. Call me your Coffee Table." He stared at the table, then at the building it was sitting in front of, and then he looked over his shoulder for possible witnesses. He decided to answer the calling. Ethan threw the wooden coffee table on his back, four legs sticking straight in the air like a taxidermied pet, and walked the remaining mile and a half home, hunchbacked. Some part of that night flashed before his eyes, at least for an instant, every time he looked at the table.

He lifted a ceramic plate and a cigar box from inside the drawer, and placed them on the old wooden table. The cigar box was holding papers and fire. And a half ounce of marijuana, stuffed inside an expired brown prescription bottle. With the precision of a thousand executions, he laid a sheet of rolling paper in the center of the plate, crumbled the herb over the paper, then, with his thumb and forefinger, he lifted the unrolled joint from the plate and centered the weed on the paper. Next, he removed a Bicycle playing card from within the cigar box. With the Queen of Hearts he scraped together the contents of the paper that had escaped from out the sides and fallen back down on the plate. He reapplied, licked the paper from left to right, and rolled.

The cigarette sat on the plate, rolled and ready to burn, while Ethan set the mood for his high. He fingered through his milk-crated record collection before settling on *Mingus Mingus Mingus Mingus Mingus*. The bass took him back across the living room, building slowly, one beat at a time. Then with the cymbals, shaking his head and spine, with their *rat-tata-ta-tat*; he danced, he funked, he moved, and then he collapsed into the couch, fingers still dancing, pulling his body forward toward the joint on the plate. *Rat-tata-ta-tat! Rat-tata-ta-tat! Rat-tata-ta-tat!* It was Jazz! America's Jazz, singing through the record. It bled through the speakers. It soaked through his pores. Ethan reached for the fire, grinding the wheel of the lighter several times until the spark turned to flame. The paper caught and he pulled the filtered air into his lungs. The tip of the joint burned orange, while his body grooved and settled into its own rhythm. Rhythm... Rhythm... Rhythm.

Ethan's head fell to his shoulder and sleep set in. Summer vacation brought new goals, creative goals: write new songs, learn Spanish, read a book, write a play. Painting always seemed cathartic, learn to paint. Surely Meramec Community College offered a class for beginning painters, ART101. Goals and hopes and desires, they all came to the forefront during his high. More often than not though, the morning would pass with a run, and the afternoon with the internet, a joint, and a nap. Evenings were set aside for Maggie. But he earned it, his mind told his body, so what. He's a teacher; three months' vacation is part of the deal, the contract, it's the reward for dealing with those kids the other nine months of the year. Tomorrow's another day, he said to himself as he drifted off to the afternoon nap, tomorrow will bring a creative burst.

The needle on the record skipped like a meter.

Scratch.

Scratch.

Scratch.

The sun was saying its slow goodnight, still hanging around, barely enough to rely on, but as the edge of the sunset poured through the French doors in the living room, Ethan woke with a peaceful heart. His cat nap had been effective. Dinner needed to be started. Maggie was less likely to complain about his level of productivity (or lack thereof) if life was easy for her when she got home. Dinner? Fish, breaded and baked. The oven needed pre-heating. One more song, he decided, one song, then cook.

Ethan blindly grabbed a record from the crate; the falling sun provided sufficient light to see but not enough to read. It hardly mattered, his collection was strong. Whatever the album, it wouldn't disappoint. He pulled the vinyl from its cover and then from its sleeve. It was Jeff Buckley; a posthumous record. Ethan could tell by the rain on the opening track. Jeff commanded the weather on the album to stop. He commanded nature, he was the band, he was god. Ethan danced again, floating on the carpet, listening to Mr. Buckley's song, "Everybody Here Wants You." He relit the cigarette and took another long drag, holding it, tasting it, letting it go. Ethan's arms relaxed and fell as he spun. He was in the moment, a boy, guided by music. The drug, the music, the sunset, together they gently lowered his guard. He raised the volume and closed his eyes so his head could flow, not *with* his torso and legs and arms, but not against them either. They were each individuals, dancing together like a group of strangers in a crowded concert, moving separately, but to the same song, forming their own dance, their own body.

Maggie managed to open the door and walk into the duplex without drawing Ethan's attention. He was lost. And she too was instantly absorbed by the moment, by the movement, by the energy. She dropped her purse and removed her blouse where she stood, one step inside the front door. She lost herself too, dancing her way toward her fiancée, softly, quietly, dancing around him, joining the concert. She wrapped her arms around his waist, startling him for a brief second, and then he laughed; partly embarrassed, partly relieved that it was her. He turned to her, draping his arms over her shoulders. Maggie took the marijuana cigarette from his lips and pulled hard on the last of it. They kissed. She removed his shirt, the skin of his chest now free to touch hers. She bent over, her ass fully on display, and set the drug onto the plate. Slowly, she unzipped her skirt, letting it slide over her curves and onto the floor. She mouthed the words to him, "How our love will blow it all away…."

Maggie flexed her hips with the snap of the snare drum, pulling him in closer to her body with each measure. They kissed with wet, open mouths. Her fingers explored the back of his head, her teeth closed on his thick bottom lip. Maggie ran the tips of her long, French manicured nails down his spine, tickling him in spots, leaving marks in others. She could be rough in the best way. She was slow with the buttons on his jeans, and quick to expose what she wanted to see. They were naked, dancing, kissing, sweating. She was wet, and he was hard. Ethan took her weight in his arms and lowered her to the carpet. In the center of the room, his body on top of hers, they danced together as one. He took control, penetrating her to the beat of each new song. Their eyes connected constantly, checking in on one other, searching for approval. She could feel his veins and he could feel her clamp down on him. Ethan pushed her arms above her head and stretched her as long and tall as her body would allow. She rolled onto him. Ethan watched as her breasts swung free and fast, her nipples erect. Maggie screamed for him. By the time they had finished the final song on the record, "You and I," had begun. It was slow and ethereal, calling to their souls. They had made love.

AUGUST 18

A streetlight stood guard directly in front of the next door neighbor's property. The light was a regular pet peeve of Ethan's, and a frequent problem when it came time for sleeping. It was a High Pressure Sodium light, which cast a wide orange glow onto the street and sidewalk, and into the rooms of the houses facing Tower Grove Park. The orange was obnoxious and unattractive to the eye; he much preferred the white street lamps of Boston or Los Angeles, cities he'd visited when traveling with Maggie for her job training conventions.

The orange light was a subconscious reminder of Ethan's first sweetheart, the girl he dated for nearly half his high school career. Christine Dunlap was her name, Ethan's first love. The love to which all other loves would later be measured and compared. The Dunlap's were an upper-middle class family; they were the ceiling of the middle class, pushing its boundaries with each annual income-tax report. Christine was raised in a brick home in Chesterfield, Missouri, just outside of St. Louis, built not two years before she was born. She had a younger sister, Julia, but there was plenty of wealth to spoil them each equally. Ethan never did learn how her father made his money, lawyer maybe, it never seemed to matter much to Christine, what kind work her father did. She was merely a product of his success, and that was just a fact of life, but she did not abuse it, or even appear to be entitled to it around others less fortunate than she. That said, she was given everything she would need to succeed on her own, she had a leg up.

For her sixteenth birthday, Christine got a car, a Pontiac Grand Am. In high school, that was the car she and Ethan spent most of their time in driving around the city. That was the car they took to the movies. That was the car that would drive them for ice cream after track meets. That was the car where they both lost their virginity; cliché, they were well aware, but a romantic cliché, and when they finished, they discussed their grandparents going through a similar rite of passage, how very American.

The car was also the location of their final night as a couple. Inside the Pontiac, Christine broke his teenaged heart. She didn't cry, he remembered that much of the event quite clearly, but her specific words and reasoning were basically a blur, an orange blur. While she was going on about wanting to be single in college, or how it would never work if they went to different schools, whatever it was she said, Ethan was staring at the dashboard of the Pontiac Grand Am. It was backlit by a hideous orange light, red orange, uncomfortable orange; it was a Halloween party every night inside that car. He had been expecting that "talk" for weeks, so when she finally worked up the courage to confront him, to let him down easy, Ethan chose to zone out. He stared at the display clock, 9:48 pm, a bright orange 9:48. Somehow, all of their joyous times together, being young and in love, group dates at various bowling alleys, making out in the back row at Crestwood Mall's movie theater, or the fucking loss of their virginity, all of those moments were smothered by one blinding memory; an irritatingly orange dashboard that read 9:48 pm.

That same nauseating shade of pumpkin poured out of the streetlight and around the edges of Maggie and Ethan's curtains, reminding him of that night inside the Pontiac Grand AM. His body shifted in his sleep, allowing the pillow he used to cover his head to fall off the mattress. Restless, and adjusting his body, his toes slipped out from beneath the covers and onto her side of the bed. It was empty. She'd tossed the duvet over exposing the bottom sheet. Without the cover, it was cold on her side, and when Ethan's foot recognized the change in temperature he twitched his eyes open, forcing them shut again the second he saw the damn orange streetlight. He reached for her, extending his arm onto her half of the bed, sliding his hand up to the pillow expecting to feel her hair but coming up empty.

"Mags?"

No answer. He moved again, tossing his body weight around the mattress more freely, and rolled over on the exposed sheet. He dragged his leg up the bed and contorted into a sort of fetal position. There was moisture. A section on the sheet was damp and he could feel it with the inner portion of his knee. Ethan stiffened with curiosity. He reached his hand down to the wet area and lightly padded the spot with his fingertips. From the touch, he could tell it wasn't water. He tapped it again, this time rubbing his thumb and forefinger together afterwards. The liquid was thick, sticky even. With his free hand, he turned on the bedside lamp to get a clearer view, to get answers. There was a circle, bright and red, where Maggie should be sleeping. Ethan looked at the blood on the tips of his fingers; with fear and protection in his voice, he called for her again, and again, there was no answer, and no other lights were on inside the duplex either. He stumbled out of bed

63

toward the bathroom and steadied himself on the doorframe, before flicking the light switch. The bathroom was clean and empty, everything in its place, towels, tooth brushes, medicine cabinet closed. But her blue nursing scrubs, the ones she usually slept in, were on the floor, crumpled the rug just outside the bathtub. What did she wear to bed? Was it the scrubs? What was she wearing? His mind tried to piece their evening together.

"Mags?" he called to her, a sense of relief now in his voice since seeing the scrubs.

No response.

He turned back to the blood stained bed, for a long moment, standing quietly, listening, thinking, his mind consumed with concern. His thoughts drifted to the most horrific of explanations: murder; was it possible that someone had broken into their home and murdered his fiancée, him sleeping through the entire event, through her struggle? Suicide; she stabbed herself, she stabbed herself and left the house to bleed out, but, no, there's no weapon, no trail of blood. Could she be bleeding to death; could she have had a cancer, or some mysterious illness that she'd been hiding from him, for years? Rationality pushed through; her period; that made sense, she was alone, outside walking, walking off the cramps.

There was a noise, a slight movement behind him, and it disrupted his silence, his worry. Ethan turned back to the bathroom and fixed his eyes on the shower curtain wrapped around the bathtub. His feet took slow steps across the cold tile floor. Reaching out, he pulled the curtain, rings sliding against the shower curtain rod. He looked down, in the corner of the tub, there was Maggie, curled up, naked, her mouth pressed against her knees. Her eyes were pink from salty tears, her face puffy. A substantial stream of blood flowed from her vagina, across the white bathtub, and down the drain, where it coated the copper pipes hiding behind the walls.

She looked up at him, somehow unable to restrain a short, sick burst of laughter. Her smile was littered with fear.

"I killed it, Eth. I'm so sorry."

AUGUST 18

    "I killed it... I killed it..." she kept repeating, staring at him, waiting for him to swoop in and rescue her, to make it all go away. She knew he couldn't. "I'm sorry, Eth," she said, over and over again. Her words shook the ground beneath him and knocked him off balance. His hip crashed into the corner of the sink counter top, he reached, blindly, for any type of support. Ethan turned and stumbled out of the bathroom. The walls began to spin in slow motion around the red dot in the center of the mattress. In an attempt to stabilize his equilibrium, he pushed the back of his wrist into his forehead, starting at the bridge of his nose and fanning out to the pressure point in his eyebrow. He had to get out. There was room to breathe outside, space to collect these dangerous thoughts. He braced himself on one of the spinning walls and jammed his feet into the running shoes, to hell with *efficiency*. He had to leave the funhouse. The old brick duplex no longer looked anything like his home. It was a dream. A nightmare. It must've been a dream, I must still be sleeping, he thought. Maggie was calling to him from deep within her cave, "I'm sorry, Eth," she kept repeating, but her voice was muffled to his ears. The sight, the red line on the white tub, the silence, it drowned him. He was underwater and her voice was nothing more than an inaudible vibration. The door slammed behind him, and he nearly fell down the stairwell, catching himself on the handrail before the last of the steps. The duplex was spinning like mad.

Ethan avoided a set of headlights as he crossed Arsenal and made his way into the park. He found his feet, they were under him, they were sturdy. The park was well lit, and the air fresh enough, cool enough to shock, and then settle, his system. Ethan took long deep breaths as his sprint steadied into a comfortable jogging pace. The pavement was solid. It steadied his legs. One foot in front of the other, smashing hard against the concrete, he ran further away from her; one foot in front of the other, trying to force the images out of his head: Maggie, tears, blood, the face she must have seen on him, the pity she sought. But try as he might, it was useless. They were stuck, clear as day, every time he closed his eyes. Flashes of the pain he assumed she must have been feeling were breaking past his ears and into his brain. He left her there, bleeding and crying, with their future being rinsed across a white cast-iron bathtub, being wiped away from existence by nothing more than a bucket of water. *I left her there*, he said to himself, ashamed. He closed his eyes, pulling tears back into his face. His thoughts streamed together, solutions, options, the right words he could have said if only he had said any words at all. *She was wrong! How could she!? I have a choice! I should've had one. I'll go back. I'll go back and tell her I have a choice and she'll listen and this will be okay. Fuck. How could you keep this from me? We're a team. We were a team! Are you okay?*

Was it mine? Fuck. What are the other secrets? Where are they hiding?

Ethan stopped running, his mind needed to catch its breath, exhausted with the array of thoughts raging behind his eyes. He grinded his wrist against his forehead again, his heart was speeding, trying to recover from the shock of her words. Ethan took a couple slower, deeper breaths, and stood erect, with his hands on the top of his head, spreading his lungs, trying to slow his pulse. Six miles had passed; he'd circled the park twice and was back at the intersection of Kingshighway and Arsenal, half a block from the duplex, from Maggie. Go home or keep running? His eyes wanted new things to look at, new attempts to sever the connection to the mind's eye, but his body wanted to quit, needed to. The red cursive letters from the Walgreens sign just across the street, the opposite direction from his home, were inviting. He wasn't ready to face her, so he turned right, and walked toward the pharmacy's empty parking lot.

At three o'clock in the morning, the inside of the Walgreens Pharmacy felt like purgatory to Ethan. The aisles were empty and it appeared the clerk had been patiently awaiting his arrival, only to dole out penance. Ethan nodded his head in her direction but she did not reciprocate. She merely glanced, continuing her three AM clerkly duties (which basically amounted to staying awake), and watched him disappear into the store.

He navigated the store swiftly, like he had somewhere else to be, cutting up one aisle and down another, knowing what to look for but not exactly where to find it. Stopping at a wall of dish soaps and detergents, he looked over the selection. After a moment or two of half-assed price comparisons, Ethan grabbed a bottle of dish soap and a plastic wrapped pack of white terry cloth. He patted the pockets on his sweats, hoping he'd remembered his wallet in the rush out the door. He did. It was in his front right, zipped up. Keys were in the left. The habitual way of leaving the duplex, keys and phone in the left pocket, wallet in the right, had paid off. Ethan was breathing less heavily now, normal even. The store was calming. His heart rate slowed. Music played from the ceiling speakers, some poppy hit with an amusing saxophone solo from years past. If this is purgatory, Ethan said to himself, limbo wasn't so bad, he could make do. Walking back through the store, on his way to the checkout, his steps were slower. He wasn't ready to leave, to face the empty parking lot and cross Kingshighway, to walk down his block with the disgusting orange streetlights and up the stairs of his brick duplex, to have a most unpleasant talk. He took the long way around and walked through the back of the store; he couldn't help but stop and laugh at the wall of condoms. It didn't make sense, had no baring really, he hadn't worn one since junior year, but still, its timing and placement were amusing to him, and so he laughed, not loudly, though he wanted to, but just a chuckle, a chortle.

He stopped again, this time staring at rows and shelves of medication: NyQuil, Advil, Pepto Bismol, pills, liquids, nasal inhalants, ibuprofen, antacids, Visine drops, decongestants and antihistamines, an icepack. But Ethan didn't see the labels or the brands, the variations in medications, not even the icepack; he saw the blue gel inside. He could taste it, its poison. He could feel the inner lining of his stomach burn and dissolve as the icepack gel slid through his intestines. He could feel the numbness the proper dosage of dextromethorphan could provide, the warm needles walking down the spine, tickling the back of the leg, settling between toes. Pill after pill, cream after cream, ointments and liquids, he stood in wanderlust at the deep stacks of medicine, wanting to travel down each of their roads. *Medicine. Medication. A way out! Relief! A cure!*

His mind took over. It ripped through the plastic wrap and cotton filter on the Tylenol PM, and shredded the foil backing on the Benadryl tabs, cracking open the child safety lock on the cough syrup and washing a dozen pills down his throat. The aisle was in disarray and he sat in the mess, among the wrappers and cardboard boxes, drinking the last of a cherry flavored bottle of Robitussin. It fell from his hand, splattering across the tile floor. He couldn't hang on any longer, his body collapsed, and his head crashed against the shelf behind him. Ethan's eyes flickered and then closed, his heart slowed, slowed. Slower, still. Slow. And finally, it stopped. It was over.

The song ended; there he stood in front of the rows and shelves of unopened medication, staring at them. He exhaled, audibly. Ethan paid the clerk for the towels and the dish soap, but the clerk was barely there, barely human, and no connection was made between them. Maybe on another day it wouldn't matter, and maybe in the grand scheme of things Ethan shouldn't have really cared one way or another. Except that he did, in that moment. In that moment he wanted the clerk, the poor clerk working the graveyard shift for pennies over minimum wage, to look him in the eye and tell him to have a nice night, to tell him that everything was going to be okay, that everything would end up alright. All he really wanted was a smile.

The automatic double doors closed behind him, and the night was cold and cruel. Ethan turned and faced his street. Where was Maggie, he wondered. Where was her mind? Was she still crying two hundred yards away on the second floor of that brick building?

The handle on the bedroom door made noise when Ethan released it, something was loose inside. He made a mental note to pull a screwdriver out from the basement storage and fix it in the morning. But Maggie was asleep and the sound of the doorknob did not wake her. She was curled, fetal, on the carpet, bundled up beneath the duvet. Ethan closed the door, being extra careful with the loose insides of the handle. Trying not to touch the cover, making every effort to let her sleep soundly, he stepped over her and walked into the bathroom. Inside, he closed the door, turned on the light, and set the Walgreens bag inside the sink. Curiosity was nagging him; he pulled back the shower curtain. No blood, just the white floor of the tub. However, the memory was there, always would be, he assumed, burned and imprinted forever. He pulled the curtain shut, quietly, softly. The emotions had drained her, he knew, but he feared the smallest noise would wake her, and if she woke, if they were to speak to one another, he would lose all hope of the night being nothing more than a terrible dream. Ethan knew it wasn't a dream, there was no doubt about it, but there was hope, there was hope that maybe tomorrow things would be less bad. As he pulled the curtain from the top, sliding each individual ring across the curtain rod, he examined the shower, his eyes trying in vain to avoid the rusty drain – not knowing whether it was healthier to say goodbye or try and block the evening out entirely.

Either way, it was futile, the nights events were done and the ramifications forthcoming. No way to set back the clock, no chance to reconsider his actions and act with strength instead of running out, no possibilities of going even further back and questioning her feelings, showing support and devotion, and making the decision together. He slid his hands along the fabric of the shower curtain in a pathetic attempt to caress something, to connect with something, anything. The fabric had never caught his eye before, but now it was so vibrant. It was thick, with asymmetric patterns, brown against white, he could see the stitching, the needle hard at work to create an artist's design. Ethan turned back to the sink, to the plastic Walgreens shopping bag. The terrycloth package ripped open easily, and he poured the soap over the center of the rag. His eyes were fighting the mirror. He knew someone would be starting back at him, someone other than Ethan Atkinson, teacher, brother, fiancé. There would be someone new, someone scorned. Fear pumped through his veins again, and he hated himself for wanting to run away a second time, first from Maggie, and now from himself. He reached out and killed the light.

      Ethan walked back to the bedroom, to the bed. While he was out running Maggie had pulled the sheets off and used an old towel to cover the stain. Hope was gone. He stepped over her once more and climbed onto the bed, he threw the towel, the cover-up towel, to the floor. The soap lathered as he worked the terrycloth against the mattress. The lather took away as much of the red coloring as the stain was willing to part with. When his hands started to cramp, he quit, he buried the towel and the rag and the sheets in a trash bag and left them in the dumpster behind their duplex, in the alley. Ethan took his pillow from atop the bed and lay down next to Maggie on the floor. He fit his body around hers, molded his shape to hers, and closed his eyes. The sun was coming up over the park and it washed out that terrible orange light from the streetlamp.

AUGUST 23

Sneakers squeaked across the hardwood floor of the gymnasium. The high pitched squeal of rubber on polished wood, the leather bound ball bouncing up and down the court, a shot too hard and too far clanking off the back of the rim, swearing, grunting; these are the sounds of the game. Eight men in a scrimmage, half of them wearing shirts, the other half skins. Russ had his shirt on and was guarding Ethan, who had the ball held tight at his hip in a triple threat position. Dipping his shoulders right for a split second, Ethan faked, used a crossover dribble, and brushed pass his defender's shoulder. Russ fell back on his heels, off balanced. Ethan took two hard dribbles with his left hand and created distance between him and his defender, when another shirt slid into the lane, help-side defense. Russ was still recovering, three feet away, and Ethan was open just inside the key; he pulled up for a fifteen foot jump-shot. It was long by a few inches, the ball rattled the rim, and the rebound was pulled down by a rival shirt.

"Fuck!" Ethan yelled.

"Aww, come on," said Lind Kirby, shaking his head.

Lind was a Skin, on Ethan's team, and he had little hesitation voicing his disapproval. It was his first week playing in their weekend "league" and it was already clear that his concept of team generally involved someone passing to him so he could make the shot. Or miss it, it didn't matter so long as he took it. Ethan spent most of the first game imagining that Lind Kirby, father to Ethan's favorite student, Jacob, had two or three great years in his entire life, most likely his sophomore and junior years of high school. That was when his looks were peaking, he probably came once or twice with a girl, and maybe he scored a few points on the basketball court too. And now, twenty something years later, he's a St. Louis County cop, lacking any imagination, and all humility. But he *was* the father of a student, and he could run up and down the court for a few hours, and that was good enough to earn an invite from Russ to play on Saturday mornings.

The Shirts crossed the three-point line and the teams switched from offense to defense.

Russ being Russ, ran his mouth. "What happened there? I gave you that one." Ethan liked Russ, on some level. But he pitied him too. Russ was the mentor, in his own mind. Russ was the leader, in his own mind. Russ was the kid who never fit in, but had too much self-confidence to let that bring him down. So he over compensated, he was bigger and louder, and more friendly than the socially accepted norms permitted. The result was a purely artificial personality and Ethan saw through it from day one, when he *showed him around* the school and basically pissed all over his turf so it was clear who had the upper hand, the seniority. But it amused Ethan. He felt badly for Russell. Ethan could see through the mask, he could see the boy inside. Russ had a good heart, he wasn't malicious; he was annoying, but he wasn't malicious. And so, more often than not, Ethan reacted with passive compassion for little Russ.

Russ stood tall near the baseline, pretending to be out of the play, pretending to relax. But he kept up the talking, "When I give you open jumpers like that you gotta nail 'em, kiddo. Can't miss the easy ones."

Ethan knew it was coming but he didn't know when, he couldn't catch up. Russ took off like a rocket from one corner of the baseline and ran beneath the basket toward the other corner. He caught the pass in stride, planted his pivot foot, squared to the rim, and took the shot.

"Boom!" Russ shouted, pumping a fist in the air. "Game! Nailed it, kiddo. Where were you?" The Shirts high-fived, the Skins lowered their heads and walked off the court, two toward the water fountain, two toward the bench to sit and recover.

"Can't shoot, can't play defense," Lind said to the floor while walking toward the fountain. "What is he an art teacher or something?" he asked one of the others. Ethan heard it, thought of giving him the finger, but figured it wouldn't help if he ever needed to name drop his way out of a speeding ticket.

"We gonna run 'em again?" Russ asked. He was shooting free-throws alone on the court. The man loved it when he was on top, he relished in his moment. "The old dog still has a few moves, huh, Kiddo?" He missed the free throw, hurried to the rebound, and lined up for another. Miss.

•

In the locker room, Ethan pulled off his shoes, tucked the laces inside, and set them in his black gym bag. His cell phone was vibrating; he removed it from the side pocket. *Maggie Cell* read across the display. Ethan let it ring, then pressed *Ignore* and tossed it back into the bag. Nothing good was going to come from anything he said to anyone. He was in a sour mood. Bad game, bad day, bad week. The constant flow of extraneous thoughts had begun to wear him down, and he'd been hoping the pickup game would relieve some of the stress, give his mind a break. The game usually served that purpose. It was a mental vacation of sorts, but his bad attitude and lack of energy, and all around general shitty play on the court just added to his frustrations. And here was Maggie, calling the moment he sat down, the first moment he could be alone and resign himself to his state. He couldn't bring himself to talk to her, not now, not yet. It was going on five days. Each time Maggie was ready to discuss what had happened, to open up, apologize, and connect with her best friend, Ethan gave the same response: not yet. Pressing *Ignore* was the safest option.

When he tossed the phone back into the gym bag, he heard the locker room door open in the distance. A few seconds later, Russ was leaning his thinning, gray haired head around a row of lockers and into the aisle where Ethan was hiding in.

"See ya next Monday, kiddo."

Ethan nodded and removed his socks, he tossed them in the bag, but Russ lingered a moment, clearly curious and looking for a talk, for a friend. "I don't know who has it harder, us getting back in gear or the kids. How"

"Yeah." Ethan forced the response, but it was polite enough.

"Every year I say this is the last one, but here I am. I keep coming back. I'm like an addict." Russ stepped fully into the isle now and adjusted the strap on his gym bag, getting comfortable. "I don't know, I guess I still get a kick out of watchin' the kids. They're probably teachin' me a thing or two too, but I aint gonna admit it. Plus we got the free gym membership and all. I'd be a fool to let that go, huh?" Russ laughed at how clever he was. Ethan had removed his shirt and draped it over his head. He was leaning back, supporting his head on the row of lockers behind him. Russ was not excellent at picking up non-verbals. Ethan did not want to talk. He did not want company. He was not capable of pulling together enough energy to make-nice and be Russ's friend.

"You okay, Kiddo? You seemed a little off your game today. I mean, I know I was guarding ya' but-"

"Fuck you."

"Whoa, easy. I'm not bustin' balls here. Just checkin' in on ya'. See if you need to talk or somethin'."

They were quiet, Ethan wanting the conversation to be over, Russ, like a dog needing to rub against its human for comfort despite having just been scolded, needed an answer.

"Kiddo. You okay?"

Ethan pulled the shirt back to uncover his eyes and rolled his head against the lockers to face Russ. "I'm good. Thank you."

Russ was unsatisfied with the response but he figured it was best not to inquire further. "I'll see you Monday, Kiddo." He'd done what he could, he reached out.

Russ's steps echoed through the empty locker room as he left. When the door closed behind him, Ethan sat forward and sighed. Finally. No phone calls. No co-workers. No responsibilities. Nothing. A deep, empty silence filled the locker room. Ethan stripped down, wrapped a towel around his waist, and slid into his shower sandals. Walking through the sour smelling locker room, his feet felt heavy and sluggish, like he was pulling them through wet cement, and his muscles and joints ached, they were sore from activity. He was starting to feel age. There was a mirror and a scale on the way to the showers and he used them. He still looked good, he thought, better than many men his age, no belly lip hanging over his towel, no major scars or obnoxious amounts of body hair, so what if he wasn't "muscular." The scale read 164lbs before the beam swayed back and forth in equilibrium. At least he had his health.

Before the entrance to the shower, along the near wall, he noticed the door to the janitor's closet was ajar. He grabbed the handle, pushed the door open and reached inside for the light switch. Apart from a mop and bucket and the usual janitorial supplies, Ammonia, Windex, shelves of toilet paper, the room was empty. He killed the light but was unable to remove his hand from the door's handle, the door remained open. Ethan stared into the dark closet, his face blank, his thoughts random and unclear. Racing thoughts, images of a busy locker room after practice, his own time in a similar locker room a decade and a half before, showering in high school in fear of every other judgmental eye, showering in college in Fusz Hall and sharing the bathroom with the fifty-five others that occupied the dormitory's sixth floor, Maggie, his Mother, what his mother would think of him, would she be proud? Would she comfort him? Would she recognize him?

Moments like these happened often, several times a month, and when they happened, they happened quickly, in flash. He could be washing dishes in his kitchen sink and the warm water and the yellow rubber gloves would take him back to his grandparent's house, standing in their kitchen as a teenage boy, on their linoleum floor, doing their dishes. He could hear the phone ring, their yellow rotary telephone that shook whenever someone would call, and from the telephone he would travel to conversations he'd had on that telephone, with old buddies and old girlfriends and their secret late night discussions about nothing, but oh how important they were, and oh how good Kelly Rena's voice sounded with the phone pressed up against his ear. Ethan remembered how he would hide at the top of the basement stairs with the door closed behind him, whispering into the handset. He often worried his grandfather would wake at night and follow the yellow cord that curled out from the base of the telephone and ended somewhere behind the basement door. He worried his grandfather would press an ear to the door and listen in on his late night conversations. And he'd be disappointed, ashamed of his grandson, of his language, the things he would say to a young girl. Then his grandfather would grab a belt and beat his legs. Ethan would drop the phone and scream in agony. And Kelly would be on the other end, listening, laughing. But those were only fears, worries. Worries he'd experienced as a young boy and recalled as an adult while drying his dishes and wearing yellow rubber gloves. Like a near death experience, his life would pass before him, a singular object recalling some distant memory and so on down the line until he snapped back to the present moment. But he enjoyed them. They made him feel like he had already lived a full life, like maybe nothing was missing after all.

Still holding the handle, the coldness of the locker room air on his bare chest brought him back to the present moment. He looked over his shoulder and listened to the empty room. The other guys had all left after the game, going back to their wives and families. Ethan flipped the light switch up again and stepped into the janitor's closet. Unsure exactly of what he was doing or what he was planning to do, Ethan bent down with one hand on the towel to keep himself covered. He was simply reacting, like a newborn or a puppy, and whatever caught his eye he would enjoy. He reached out with his free hand toward the cleaning supplies, toward the bottle of Ammonia, and removed its cap. Ethan held the bottle to his nose and sniffed. It was intense. The smell was so strong and sudden, knocking his head back, thrusting his body erect. He tried to collect himself, securing his towel from falling and exposing his naked body. Above his head on a shelf, there were packs of brown, single fold, paper towels. Carefully, he slid the top three out from their wrapper, making sure not to disrupt the rest of the packet, and held the paper towels over the open top of the Ammonia bottle. Ethan turned the bottle over until the paper was saturated, gripped the wad of wet brown paper in his hand, and pressed it to his nose and mouth, inhaling deeply. Water flooded his eyes from the inside out, and the whites instantly turned bloodshot. His heart pounded beneath his chest and it felt good so he inhaled again, pulling harder than the time before. And again. And again. He lost count at seven when he crashed to the floor. The bottle fell from his hands and emptied itself around him. Ammonia and adrenaline were working together inside his body. Blood was rushing rapidly through his veins, lifting the skin on his neck with each pulse. His heart was pumping at full force and each beat felt like a strobe light washing him in the brightest, most gorgeous light of the afterlife, then leaving him in the cold lonesome darkness of hell. Then light. Then dark. Then light. And so it continued with each contraction of the muscle beneath his chest. There were needles in his toes, thousands of needles, he'd lost control, he was aware he'd lost control, but he was too weak, too overpowered by the drug, to fight back. The simple act of covering himself with the towel took an inordinate amount of effort, so he lay there still, naked, coming in and out of the strobe light, staring at the pubic hair inches below his belly button that became exposed with the fall.

The needles faded. Ethan flexed his bicep several times just to see if his arm would receive the brains message. Three minutes had passed since he opened the door to the janitor's closet. Objects regained their focus. Ethan pawed at the walls, though they seemed to float just out of reach, until he managed to pull himself up off of the floor slowly. His body felt heavier than before, he thought, heavier than after the basketball game and twice as unbalanced, he struggled to hold himself upright. He was sure the scale would read differently if he stood on it now. Ethan took deep breaths again, this time with clean air, and tried to calm himself. Panic had quickly replaced the strobe light and he scolded himself for being so stupid as to do *drugs* on school grounds! He wasn't thinking clearly and it made him angry.

Looking around the room, the janitor's closet had become a crime scene. He cursed in whispers, knowing he was alone, but for how long? His feet were wet, and after a full minute of consciousness, he could smell the chemical, it overpowered the closet, and he was sure it was spreading throughout the entire locker room. Ethan scrambled to clean up the mess. The brown paper towels were shit for soaking up so much liquid, and the mop, he reasoned, might lead a trail of evidence back toward him, to his being there. The police would lift prints from his classroom and match them to the mops wooden stick, they'd question him in front of the students, the students would lose their trust in him, their love for him. He'd go prison.

Ethan looked out into the locker room again to be sure he was still alone and then closed the closet door. He removed the towel from his waist and threw it on the ground. On his hands and knees, naked, he covered every inch of the floor with the towel. As he settled further into his body and the drug finished, his nerves began to emerge. Only the nerves were less about fear, fear of the future or getting caught, and instead seemed to be associated with a sense of surprise. In a peculiar way, he was actually pleased with himself. His new, and unexplainable actions, rendered him excitable. What else was he capable of? What was next?

When he'd finished, he wiped the door handle of any prints and left it open to diffuse any remnants of the smell. Clinging to the wet, black towel, he stood naked in the locker room contemplating his next move. He was still wobbly, and like a blind man in an unfamiliar place, he used the wall to guide him toward the showers. The black towel was dragging on the floor behind him, like a child with a blanket.

The water was hot on his skin but it felt safe. There was an urge to vomit but he pushed it down; his throat and eyes were burning but at least it was something, at least he was feeling again. It had been nearly a week with hardly any feelings at all. Lowering

81

his head and letting the shower massage his scalp, he looked down at his body for answers, he thought of the stories his body could tell, the life he had led, the ground his feet had gripped, his penis, his hands. The water turned his skin red from the heat. He felt a peculiar confidence, like a criminal driving across the border into Mexico. He pressed the black towel to his face once more and pulled air into his lungs.

AUGUST 23

He wasn't ready to go home. Maggie was home and he was sure she'd want to *talk*. She was ready to *talk*, had been since she woke up the morning after. It was the first time, as far back as Ethan could remember, that Maggie was up and out of bed before him. She made coffee that morning; brought it to him on the floor, where he was still sleeping, wrapped in the covers. Apparently, overnight, Maggie had processed everything she'd needed to process and was ready to hear how Ethan felt about the abortion. But that was the problem, he didn't yet know. Ethan ignored her that morning, cold shoulder, one word answers (he didn't even drink from the cup of coffee), and for the next five days he was on a rollercoaster, talking himself into and out of anger, working himself up over her undeniably selfish act, and moments later convincing himself that he was making too big a deal out of it, that nothing *really* happened, and he should be strong and move

83

forward. He'd decided to sleep on the couch the next night. Maggie didn't object. She started coming home late, missed consecutive dinners. No matter, Ethan had stopped cooking them to begin with. Deep threads of hate were weaving through their every fiber. They lost communication and trust in an instant, and while both were aware of the mistrust and general negative current flowing throughout their lives, they weren't yet equipped with the skills to overcome it or, in Ethan's case, even talk about it.

His car was the only one in the Park View Elementary parking lot; assurance that, since Russ left, he had been alone in the locker room. Ethan put his gym bag in the trunk, started the car, and instead of turning right to head back towards his Tower Grove duplex, he decided to make a left, and cut across Musick Road and drive through Grant's Farm. The gas light was on. It had come on earlier in the morning while on his way to play basketball, but he was running late then and decided not to fill up. Now, however, there was no rush at all, and the Sinclair station was at the bottom of the hill, so he made a slight detour.

When Ethan was still a boy, long before his grandparents passed, the Sinclair Gas Station attendant would come to the car door, drop his head down into the drivers-side window and, with a smile, ask, "Filler' up?" Ethan liked this. The Sinclair stations were the last to hang on to the old American tradition, and though they quit going that extra mile several decades earlier, the green dinosaur on their logo reminded him of his grandfather, of his grandfather's 1983 black Crown Victoria with maroon felt interior, and he looked back fondly.

Ethan watched the man inside the stations window, behind the counter. He didn't even have his name sewn in cursive letters above his breast pocket. He was sitting down on a stool, watching a small TV. It disgusted him, he felt sad for the countries direction, we'd become lazy, he thought to himself, and he feared the cultural hole we'd been digging might be too deep to climb out of.

As the numbers scrolled higher and higher on the pump's meter, Ethan reached below his seat and popped the trunk. He wanted more, he wanted comfort. Time moved so fast. Just yesterday he was sitting in the back seat with his sister, in this same filling station, while grandma and grandpa listened to Paul Harvey on an AM channel. *What had happened? Where did it all go and how did it all die out so fucking quickly!?* He slammed the trunk. The towel was already soaking wet from cleaning the Ammonia, but it made no difference. Pulling a section of it out from the gym bag, he rolled the towel around his fist. Then, taking the gun from the gas tank, he squeezed two quarters worth of unleaded into his hand before hanging it back in its holster. The credit card processed and he rejected an offer for receipt. With the gym bag in the passenger seat and the towel sticking out of the bag, he drove down Musick Road.

The sky held deep shades of green and blue, and the clouds were heavy above his head as he cruised through the tree-lined street, up and down the hills, multiple subdivisions opening up on each side of the road. He pressed the towel against his face for brief seconds between passing cars. The fumes of gasoline were so overpowering that he was forced to roll down the windows to maintain consciousness. This would be his goal, he'd decided, to maintain this new high, to test the boundaries without raising red flags or causing concern, to fit seamlessly into society, but to do it on another level, a higher level. If he could accomplish this, he could see through life's bullshit, he might even find a solution to his problems at home, he could, maybe, accept Maggie again, understand her, support her even.

The humidity was thick and it was coming in through the driver side window. He looked at the sky again; the green clouds were rolling. A summer storm was nearby. When he reached the end of Musick road, the light at the Gravois intersection was red, and he stared past the chain link wall into the southern border of Grant's Farm. The Farm was named after the eighteenth President, Ulysses, who lived there in a cabin nearly a century before. Now, it was a wildlife preservation property of sorts, open to the public. On a field trip last spring he took the students on the train ride through the Farm. They were arms reach from bison, deer, cattle and zebras. "Zebra's in Missouri!" he heard one of his students shout.

He'd made less than a dozen visits to the Farm in his lifetime, mostly for school field trips. Never once, he thought, had his grandparents taken him and Rachel there. They were old, and therefore any activity that forced them outside of the house wore them down, taking a year or two off their lives. They were lame, even for the elderly. Mr. and Mrs. Atkinson, John's parents, didn't want another set of kids running around, begging to be taken care of. Hell, they were sixty-plus years old, but they were obligated. What other choice did they have? They took Eth and Rach to the movies occasionally, but never to a museum, never to a ball game, and certainly never to Grant's Farm.

There was an Elk grazing near the fence while Ethan waited for the stoplight to change. Its antlers were large and full of fuzz. Ethan watched as it picked blades of grass by the mouthful, so peaceful, so delicate, but also so strong. It was a giant animal, male probably, and he was free within the confines of that fence, didn't seem to have a care in the world. Ethan honked his horn; he wanted the Elk to know he was there, to know someone was watching. The Elk lifted its head, its huge and heavy head, antlers and all, supported by its wide muscular neck, and looked with his massive round eyes directly across the street at Ethan. Ethan had gotten what he wanted and it scared him. The two men, survivors of evolution, locked on to one another and connected. They were each waiting for the other to break eye contact, and for a moment, they existed as equals, equal forms of living breathing matter. He thought of Ernest Hemmingway and Maggie's father, Rich, both *men's men,* and both avid killers of wild game. He thought of hunting shows on cable TV, and the camouflage get-up they'd all use to hide behind. How could they kill this? Sure, the thought crossed his mind, but to pull the trigger after staring into this animal's eyes? How? He knew the power the gun would give, the dominance over any species, but to watch the life disappear and the heart stop beating and to think about this poor Elk's children wondering why Daddy never come home, heaven forbid they were the ones who actually found the body; it was all too much, too cruel.

The car behind Ethan politely tapped its horn several times. He looked in his rearview mirror and then at the light, it had turned green, and the Elk had sprinted away. It's working, he said to himself. The gasoline had made him aware, it got him thinking. He felt like a wise old Indian, smoking the pipe for a purpose. Ethan made a left turn at the bottom of the hill and then into the Grant's Farm parking lot.

Like a dog on a scent, Ethan pulled several quick sniffs of the gasoline fumes into his nose and lungs before tucking the towel back into the gym bag and the gym bag back into the trunk. His hair was still wet and slicked back from the post-basketball-game-shower, but he liked it that way, it kept the longest strands from brushing against his eyeballs.

Families were exiting Grant's Farm in droves. The clouds caused the temperature to dip and the people heeded the warning. After the spring's wicked batch of tornados, everyone was on guard, waiting for the next big natural disaster. Parents quickly removed their kids from strollers and placed them in car seats, while grandparents struggled to get themselves into minivans. And Ethan was among them, in the crowd but not a part of it, walking in a drunken peaceful daze, floating above it all.

Standing on the bridge, overlooking the creek at the entrance to the Farm, he noticed a beautiful Weeping Willow tree swaying in the breeze. On his tip toes, he reached his hand out over the ledge, allowing his fingertips to caress its long green leaves. While in this state, with his mind chemically altered, he could be open, he could appreciate the world around him. The trees suddenly contained so many more colors and the wooden planks below his feet were unique and individual, they too were once trees, and now, with the help of creative mankind, the planks came together to form a beautiful and functional bridge for everyone to enjoy. People pushed past him on the bridge, some saying *excuse me*, some angry with his impediment to their destination. But he ignored them all. He was with nature, fully embracing whatever it was his mind wanted to embrace.

As he made his way farther into the park he was struck by a bright red balloon. It was a standard red rubber balloon, filled with helium and adorned with a long white string, but it was just that that made it so attractive; it's simplicity. It was as if the balloon had been plucked from a young child's drawing and brought to life right there in front of him. It bounced left and right in the air, always fighting to climb higher and higher into the stormy sky. But it couldn't. Its white string was a leash and the leash was attached to the wrist of a small boy. A gust of wind blew from the trees, tugging the balloon in yet another direction, and sending chills up Ethan's arms. He stopped walking and stared into the eyes of the boy, hoping to connect with him the same way he'd done with the Elk just minutes before. Ethan was on a quest. A quest to connect with every living being that would have him. The boy obliged. And for a moment that seemed to last an eternity, the two humans, one a grown man, the other still a child, became one. Their energies exchanged and they were forced to acknowledge each other. Ethan Atkinson could feel it. He felt genuinely connected to another human being, to a stranger no less, and it was magnificent.

The boy smiled at Ethan and it hit him like a fist to his stomach, sucking all the air from his gut and lungs. He wanted to keep the boy; he wanted the boy to be his, so he could replicate that feeling over and over again, each and every day. That boy made him feel alive in a way he'd hope to someday feel with children of his own. The feeling caused so much joy, his heart swelled so large, that it hurt. It had to hurt. The purity of the boy's smile filled him with so much pleasure he could barely allow himself to enjoy it because he knew, at any moment it would be gone, ripped away from him, washed down a bathroom drain.

The boy's mother took her son's hand and they walked away, toward the bridge, toward the parking lot, pulling the red balloon that was tied to his wrist along with them. Ethan ran to the spot where the boy had been standing with his mother, desperately wanting to hang onto the feeling that the boy had just given him, but there was nothing left to cling to, nothing but a memory.

Ethan turned in every direction, desperately needing to know where the boy had come from. What was his source of bliss, how did he remain so childlike, where did he find that simple red balloon? There was a gift shop, and inside behind the windows of the store, there were children and toys and balloons of every color! He pressed his face to the glass and watched the happy families smile. He watched as one father put his daughter on his shoulders, her legs dangling on each side of his chest. He watched a mother run her nails through her toddler's long, thin hair. Ethan wanted all of them. He wanted to teach them, to hold them, to laugh and play with them. The window he'd been pressing his face against began to fog over from his breathing.

AUGUST 23

&

SEPTEMBER 12

"Where the fuck have you been?" She said with her legs crossed and a lit cigarette puffing smoke out from between her middle and index fingers. "Why weren't you answering your phone?"

Ethan let the heavy door slam behind him, encouraged it even. The mirror in the entry way, hanging beside the doorframe, rattled against the wall. His hands were full: gym bag in one, a plastic shopping back in the other. Ethan was startled to see her sitting there on the couch, waiting for him like a disappointed parent whose teen had just broken curfew. Maggie was silent, anticipating an answer, and her impatience was threatening, the way she sucked the cigarette's smoke in with force, her calf bouncing against her knee, restless. She was looking for a fight and he wasn't about to back down. "I said, why didn't you answer your phone?" There was bitterness and anger in her voice, it radiated from her pores. Pausing in his tracks, he took a deep breath to collect himself. A smile formed at his lips, the battle ground was stirring. He knew his appearance and overall functionality were muddled from repeated use of the black towel inhaler he'd been carrying around all afternoon, but she had no way of knowing that. If he was going to fly under the radar at home, maintain his higher consciousness without judgment or persecution, he'd have to be cautious around Maggie. He disregarded her, not to prevent the fight but to prolong it, to dig further beneath her skin, and when the time was right, when he was ready, they'd have it out.

"Where have you been?" she pressed and grew louder as he stared off in silence. "Ethan, do not fucking ignore me. I'm still you're fiancée. We need to talk about what happened."

But he did ignore her. He wanted to ignore everything that conflicted with his mental bliss for long as he possibly could. Looking at the floor, or the wall, or the coffee table – he couldn't bear to look at her for fear of what he might do – he moved around the room like he had an agenda, a check list to complete. The gym bag reeked of gasoline so he buried it in the hall closet. Keys go on the hook. Wallet, phone: bedroom dresser. The other bag, the plastic shopping bag with the Grant's Farm logo printed its side, left him puzzled. He hadn't planned on sharing its contents with Maggie. The Grant's Farm bag was meant to be hidden, like a valuable baseball card, in a box below the bed or between the rafters in the attic. But the duplex had no attic, and Maggie had marched off the couch and was now standing between him and the bedroom.

"Where have you been?" she said slowly, preparing to erupt. Maggie's face was red with fury. "Where have you been all day and night?" she demanded.

For the first time since he found her in the bathtub and learned of the aborted baby, he looked her square in the eyes. "I played ball. And then I went shopping."

Maggie looked down at the bag, taking her curiosity in a new direction.

"What did you do?" she said looking back up at him. She was close enough to see the bloodshot veins in his eyes and the red, tender skin around his nostrils. "Why do you smell like gas?"

Ethan stood over her, motionless, emotionless, gripping the handle of the bag as tightly as his fist would allow. She lunged for the bag, ripping the plastic and leaving shreds of its handles in his hand. Like a child on Christmas she tore through the bag, only she wasn't happy, she was distraught, blinded by her own anger and sadness. With pieces of the bag scattered on the floor, Maggie held the contents in her hand, the contents Ethan wanted so desperately to hide but had stupidly forgotten in his drunken gasoline high.

It was a mobile. A baby's crib mobile. With her hands trembling, barely able to hold the mobile box, she looked up at him with utter confusion. She was frozen, attempting to comprehend why he would make such a purchase. What kind of man would make such a horrific practical joke at his fiancée's expense? Was that what it was, a practical joke, she wondered. She hated him. Searching his eyes for an explanation, her emotions overtook her, forcing tears to swell out and over her eyelids. And in his numbness, his expressionless face, she saw the torment that had crippled him. She saw what she had done and it hit her hard and fast. Their lives were forever changed by her actions. Their team, somehow, down one member. In that instant, a giant spotlight shone brightly on the ever-expanding hole that was eating away at their love.

She exploded, slapping Ethan's face first, and then his chest and neck. He flinched but made no attempt to defend himself or prevent her attack. He expected it. He wanted it. Touch. Connection. His skin stung and it felt fantastic, it was fulfilling. Maggie grabbed his arm, his hand still clutching the plastic from the bag, and buried her nails deep into the skin on the tender underside of his forearm. Showing signs of strain across his brow, tense creases forming, a vein coming to life down the center of his forehead, Ethan stared into her, trying to find the girl he once loved. He looked past the venom in her eyes, hoping to see remnants of a nurturing soul, one who would never act with ill intent, never lash out at the ones she loved. He searched for the woman who was careful with his feelings, who had to whisper *I love you* with her lips pressed against his ear, each night before they slept. Where was the friend with the sensitive heart, the soul mate with whom he agreed to start a family, to mother a child? Challenging her with his glare, she could only respond by forcing his flesh deeper beneath her nails.

The pain reached a threshold and he tore his arm from her grip. Warm blood moved like an insect, slowly crawling down toward the wrist. If she was no longer there behind those eyes, the girl who took his heart into her hands and claimed to love him forever, if she was no longer present, then why restrain? He *could* fight back, beat this strange demon out of his fiancées body. Grabbing her shoulders, he tossed her aside, violently, and picture frames rattled when her back collided with the wall.

"Why did you take my kid," he said, moving in on her, wrapping his hands around her shoulders again. "Why..? Why..?" He shook her with each question, expecting the answer to fall out. "Why did you kill my kid?" he said again, dominating her with his size. Tears were flowing like a flash flood down the sides of her face. Her chest was blotchy red from emotions pushing out against her skin.

"I didn't want it!" she finally screamed, "I don't know how to be a mother."

Maggie's words took all his strength away. His hands fell off her shoulders and he backed away from her.

"I didn't want it," she said again as she lowered her head and continued to cry, no longer fighting back the tears. "I couldn't do it, Eth. I got scared." The words were barely audible through her sobbing. Her feet gave into the weight of her body and she crumbled to the floor.

Ethan picked the mobile off of the floor. On the box, were pictures of the various farm animals that would hang and spin as the mobile played gentle music. He wiped the box clean of any dirt and dust it may have gathered during their fight, running the tips of his fingers over the baby deer. Several drops of blood fell from his forearm and onto the farm animals. He was exhausted, beaten raw by emotion, and so was she. With the mobile in his hand, he walked away from his fiancé.

In the bedroom, standing over Maggie's side of the bed, he pulled the covers off, then the sheets, exposing the faded blood stain on the mattress. He stood above it, in a daze, wishing it could talk, wishing he could call upon it for guidance. Ethan climbed onto the bed, one limb at a time, and laid his face next to the spot. Stunned by the loss of something he never had, he was lost, with nothing left to cling to. Somehow, when the fetus died, so did a part of Ethan, and certainly, so must have a large part of Maggie.

•

He looked up from the spot, Maggie was standing in the door way, fresh faced and clean, resolved with the kind of help only time can provide. The bedroom was bare, stripped of the things that once made it her home. The large red painting, with the black across its middle that hung above their bed, her college art project, was no longer there. It was packed away with the rest of her things, jewelry, candles, make-up; her clothes gone from the closet.

"I need to be away from you," she said, taking her engagement ring off of her finger and placing it on the corner of the mattress. "I'm not happy here, with you."

She was so strong, he thought, to move on without him, and to do it so quickly. Not even a month had passed.

SEPTEMBER 18

      The Royale was a dive. It never wanted to be a dive, a place for patrons with skin like an alligator and dark circles pulling beneath their eyes to come and forget about their shitty ten hour work day and their shittier life choices. No, The Royale had higher hopes for itself. Which is probably why it attracted the people it did, they were the same; dreamers who woke up too soon, and lovers left holding the pieces of their broken hearts.

      There were glass brick windows along the wall opposite the bar. They were old with yellow stained grout holding the blocks together. It felt like a seedy motel bathroom in a Hitchcock flick, if something was behind the window, you could see it, but there was no telling what it was. The color scheme had a cheap Mardi Gras effect: orange on one wall, purple on the ceiling, and yellow behind the bar. And it was bright. Too fucking bright. No one would ever tell stories of how they got drunk and hooked up with someone they met at The Royale because the lights were always on, always illuminating dark corners, always shinning on the ugly facial features people wished they could hide, a hook nose or a lazy eye lid, crooked teeth, receding hair lines, a zit so white and ripe for popping. It was as if the electrician forgot to install dimmers, and instead of fixing his mistake, he managed to talk the proprietor into leaving the bar looking like high noon all night, every night. And in the spirit of going the extra mile, if for some reason a customer had trouble signing the receipt on their tab because they were blind drunk or just blind from the afore mentioned obnoxious lighting, they could see their bill with the candles that were spread across the entirety of the bar.

But for Ethan, it was close to home, they served a fine rotating selection of draft beers, and in effort to be better than what it was, The Royale had a mile long "specialty drink" list, crafted from a mixologist's wet dream.

Ethan drank at The Royale three times a week since accepting his position at Park View Elementary. While what he drank varied depending on his mood, the amount never did, two drinks, no more, no less. Two drinks. That was the number that kept him in balance. Two maintained mutual respect with the alcohol, they could enjoy each other's company without ill effect. Plus, Maggie expected him to be home before she was, to have someone welcome her with kisses and attention, and to cook for her. She wouldn't understand a man's desire to Barfly. It was beyond her, the same way the desire for a woman to pass time with idle bullshit chatter was beyond him. So Ethan kept the drinks, even his visit to the bar, a secret. To be shared only with the bartender and the twenty feet of oak between them.

Ethan liked to judge the others at the bar, to feel superior to them. He didn't like that he judged, but the judging, the assumptions on people's lives based on nothing more than personal

97

appearance and first impressions, excited him. Tattoos and piercings meant unemployment, or if employed, the job certainly wasn't benefiting society in any statistically measurable way. If the man at the end of the bar wore a suit, then he hated his job, hated his wife, and more than likely hated his mother for sticking around all those years while his father beat the shit out of her, night after night. The two kids taking shots in the corner were destined for mediocrity, with their khaki pants and new balance shoes, they'd probably become managers of the cell phone store where they currently worked because, hey, the commissions are great.

He judged and judged, knowing it was wrong, knowing he was wrong about the people and his assumptions of their lives. It was all wrong. But it was a game and every detail opened a Pandora's Box of personal history. While it was a fun game to play, he played alone, often wondering what his subjects were thinking of him, wondering if they too were putting him down so that their beer would taste a little better, a little colder, just like his.

Ethan stared into the bottom of his second drink, a beer, some local brewery. The last of his ale had formed a ring of bubbles and he swirled them around the floor of his pint glass, wanting to order another. There were a few people in the bar, more than usual for Thursday, and the DJ, DJ 44, appropriately named after the interstate running east and west through St. Louis (appropriate because he was large enough to occupy all four lanes himself), had just started "spinning" on his laptop. Bored and feeling an itch for destruction, Ethan removed the coaster beneath his glass and tore off a sliver of the thin cardboard. He took the slice of cardboard and rested it gently across the center of the candle holder, watching the coaster heat up and change form, and eventually collapse into the candle, slowly turning into ash. Ethan waved his hand over the candle to diffuse the smoke and the smell.

He was ready for a third. And why shouldn't he have it? He was a man, earned a decent wage, was clearly not near intoxication, and if even if he was, he was walking home. And Maggie wasn't around. There was no need to rush home and feed her. She'd been gone for six days. For six days he waited for her to come back, suitcase in one arm and an apology in the other, but it wasn't going to happen. He'd quit on the idea of their making up, at least the happy fantasy version, where she would say, "I was wrong, you were right," and they'd make love until the morning sun poked through the trees in the park across the way. So fuck it, why not? Order a third, a fourth even.

"Bourbon. Rocks, please."

He held the whiskey in his mouth, on his tongue, and even though it burned his taste buds the way cheap whiskey often does, it also made him feel like a man. Still young by life expectancy standards, and not yet sporting any grays, he often felt not more than a few years older than his students. But whiskey, oh whiskey, how it made him feel like putting on a necktie and kicking back in a leather chair, listening to a record or two, while reading the paper. The kids running around in the other room, the wife in an apron. Whisky made him feel like it was 1952, like he was the man with the slick haircut in the LIFE magazine advertisement. *Whiskey: a time honored remedy for the battered soul.* Who cares if he didn't have the tie or the kids or the wife to fill the apron? He had the bar, and that was enough. Man, bar, whiskey. Anything else would lead to bad decisions.

But misery craves company. That's why he was drinking in The Royale to begin with. It was more comforting to drink with strangers than it was to drink at home alone, staring off into the corners of his duplex. He was hiding in public. He didn't want to be alone, and he most certainly did not want to share his pain or shoulder some other poor sap's burden. Rather, he was craving miserable company in hopes that, by reflecting each other's depressions, they could somehow bring each other peace and understanding. The hiding in public was an act of reaching out. Hiding, but desperately wanting to be found.

Somewhere between his fourth and fifth drink, a bundle of red hair walked in and sat at the other end of the bar. Red had a familiar face but he couldn't quite place it. Ethan watched her scribble words onto a cocktail napkin, scraping the fallen pieces of her red hair back behind her ears. He played his game of judgment on her, and somehow she came out unscathed. She was neither basket case nor whore - her face was too soft, it lacked the wear and tear of hard living. Definitely not unemployed, though he'd wager a tattoo was being covered somewhere. She looked well read, perhaps a college graduate who'd chiseled her own niche in the world. She might even have money, money from selling the poems she scribed on drink napkins at dingy bars near Tower Grove Park - written in Middle America's lonely bars, and published for the world to succumb to her greatness. He wanted these things for her, this personal success.

"Do you know her?" Ethan asked the bartender. The bartender looked in Red's direction, then raised an eyebrow, and nodded. "What's her name?"

"I'm not doing the work for you." The bartender said, tossing a towel over his shoulder. "You wanna talk to her, buy her a drink,"

•

After finishing the round he purchased for her, Red bought one for Ethan, and they decided to move outside to the patio where they could talk more intimately. Under a propane heat lamp he sat parallel to her, with the outside of his right knee brushing against the outside of hers. Their conversation had breezed quickly through the bullshit stage of introductory small talk –

"Can I buy you a drink?"

"That's fine but I'm not going to blow you tonight,"

"How about tomorrow?"

Beat.

Neither flinched.

He started again, "I was just looking for a chat. I was hoping you'd be more interesting than the bowl of beer nuts I've been fidgeting with over there, which, you clearly are. Plus everyone else in this bar is an asshole."

"Red wine will do just fine."

– And settled into something a little warmer, amorous, territory that might be breached on a third date.

"No, not at all! See, these kids are fucking smart," Ethan said. "They're little sponges. And they've got so much expression inside them that they're dying to get out but they don't know how to do it, or they don't feel like they're allowed," he said, shifting forward in his chair.

Red didn't mind that their bodies were touching, neither did Ethan. And even though it could be argued that they were just knees, (knees that were grinding and shifting, jockeying for position, always maintaining contact) there was a clear sexual exchange occurring between the fibers of their pant legs. While fellatio may have been off the table for the night, there was definitely an opening in the future.

"But it's tough, ya know?" he continued. "Half the time I doubt I'm making any impact on their lives at all. Like, when they go home and mom and dad say 'How was your day?' What are they thinking? I know how I was at that age. I would think about who I sat next to at lunch, or what girls I was passing notes with, or recess."

"You were a note passer, huh? A real ladies man in your younger days?" she said. Red grinned as she took a sip of her wine, as if winking with her smile.

Ethan never broke stride. He had a message and he was intent on delivering. It's part of what made him so good at his job, his passion. "The SE kids are different though. They don't have the luxury of looking normal, or acting normal, and making friends like you and I could. Some of them do, some aren't so bad, but... some of the others..."

Ethan looked across her face, her eyes, lips, to see if she was still with him. Red had her attention fixated on his mouth, interested and waiting, wanting more.

"You remember what it was like at that age, right?" he asked but continued before she could answer. "If your shorts aren't the right height, you can't take two steps without worrying what everybody is thinking about your legs, or your style, the way you walk." She laughed a little, thinking of her own silly teenage insecurities. "Right, but see, this isn't their shorts. It's their speech. Or the pace at which they have to learn, or the pills they have to take so they don't have a fucking manic fit during gym class."

Their knees had separated. Both Red and Ethan were sitting taller, less relaxed than moments before. "You're not saying anything," he said, brushing off a wrinkle or wiping some imaginary dirt off his jeans. She smiled at him without opening her mouth. Neither of them had words to justify why kids get shit on like that. Their own problems suddenly felt smaller.

"What's with the old lady ring?" she asked. Maggie's engagement ring, now strung from Ethan's necklace, poked out from beneath his shirt. He tucked it back in before responding.

"It was my Grandmothers. My mom used to wear it," he said.

She knew there was more to the story but figured this was neither the time nor place to fiddle with raw nerves. She pulled her large mass of hair up with both arms and wrapped it into a pony tail.

102

"Do you have a dog?" Ethan cocked his head to the side with curiosity as he asked. Something about the way she moved, throwing her hair up in that manner, had triggered a thought in his mind. She shook her head 'no' before finishing the last of her wine.

"I've seen you in the park, haven't I?" It was more of a statement than a question. "You looked familiar but I didn't know how or where until now. I've seen you at Tower Grove, playing with the dogs, right?"

"You've been watching me?" She wasn't angry. In fact, it appeared the accusation of voyeurism turned her on more than anything else.

"No. Not watching. Not anyth-"

"Relax. I'm fucking with you. I live over here. I'm on Iowa."

"Iowa," Ethan said, raising his eyebrows. "Over in the state streets? You're a tough chick."

"It's not that bad." She reached down and began searching through her purse.

"Yeah, Benton Park's not *that* bad," Ethan said without hiding his sarcasm.

While most South St. Louis criminals had dissipated in recent years, Benton Park seemed to remain the refuge for the persecuted convict. It was as if Gravois Road was the proverbial line in the sand. Sure there were tough neighborhoods throughout St. Louis, rundown buildings with plywood window panes, and spray paint tagging for curtains, but South City was growing, climbing out of its oppression. Young people, artistic minded people, whites, gays, and post-grads, were all moving into the red brick townhouses. And the blacks, the blue collars, the families that paid with food stamps, those who'd spend decades in the area and called it home, were all run out. Like a packet of ketchup squished by a passing boot, they splattered across town. But their

103

backs were against the wall and the wall was the river, the mighty Mississippi, and they held tight to their Benton Park Bungalows, reminding the tourists of their influence and their culture and their presence.

"Yeah, smart ass," she said. "Benton's *not* that bad. I'll show you sometime… Unless, of course, you're too scared." She winked at him. He smiled.

Truthfully, he was scared. Even after living in the Tower Grove Park Neighborhoods for nearly a decade (Tower Grove South was rough, but it was widely considered a safe enough neighborhood to raise a family), whenever he'd walk from his car to his front door, he still carried his keys between his knuckles so they'd act like tiny knives if he ever had to start swinging.

"You're not scared, are you?"

He shook his head and sipped the bourbon.

When she was finished digging through her purse she revealed a small vial the size of a bullet, and removed from the vile a small amount of cocaine. She inhaled quickly and dusted her nostrils clean; the whole thing was as simple as wiping a runny nose with a tissue, or reapplying lipstick. "I'm in the park all the time. I've probably seen you in there too."

She was so casual, so nonchalant about it. She was carrying a felony in her purse, and now in her nose, and she didn't so much as blink. Ethan looked down at her hands; they were outstretched over his lap and she was presenting the bullet, giving him permission to do the same, to *take it easy*.

He took the vial from her hands and noted how cold her fingers were in contrast to his. It was chilly outside, even under the propane heat lamp, but her fingers might as well have been blue. She smiled when he accepted. After three glasses of red wine, her teeth were stained.

"You know we've been talking all this time and I don't even know your name," she said.

"Ethan."

"Tammy."

Misery craving company.

OCTOBER 4

Blood was rushing to his cock, it was embarrassing, it was painful. His penis and testicles were forced into his underwear like three hunks of flesh colored Play-Doh jammed into a yellow plastic container, and spilling out over the edges. And one hunk, the biggest hunk, was drying out and getting hard inside the jar, crushing anything in its path. Ethan wanted to adjust and spread his legs, air everything out, but if he moved he feared she might stop, and he didn't want to send the wrong signal. He also didn't want her to feel the throbbing erection that was developing on account of her hands placement across his inner thigh.

Ethan turned his head a bit to see her face with the corner of his eye. She was watching the show. She was captivated by the performance on stage, the actors, *the theatre*. Even though she was touching him on the softest part of his legs, her intent wasn't sexual. She was being loving, sharing a moment, subconsciously, with the new man in her life.

He was sure Tammy could feel his femoral artery pumping gobs of blood to his pelvis, that she could feel him, alive in her hands. It felt good to share that tenderness, but he was terrified that if she glanced down at his crotch she might think the worst of him. *What kind of man gets an erection at Shakespeare; a black box production in a room with only 49 other people, at that?! It's not like we're at the fucking Globe, for Christ's sake.* The thoughts she could be having tormented him.

Eventually he gave into the touch, as she ran the underside of her fingernails along the inseam of his black dress slacks. It was affectionate, and it was new. This new body, this new hand, new life, it was all so foreign. Tammy was firm. Where Maggie wanted to caress the skin, Tammy wanted to get beneath it, bury herself inside and make a home, build a fire, and swim in his veins like they were wild rivers. That connection, that depth to her core, and the strength in her touch made Ethan feel safe. She made him feel warm and the thought of spending the night alone, without her hand pressed against him was terrifying. He needed that body, he needed her beneath his skin, to comfort him and show him how easy the future was going to be.

As King Lear moved stage right to deliver his aside, Ethan pulled his eyes away from Red and back onto the stage. The old man spewed passion with each word of his monologue. It fascinated Tammy, and she looked on with eager anticipation, her hand stopped and rested on the top of Ethan's quad. With the pressure in his pants subsiding, he took her soft forearm into his hand, sliding down to her wrist, and placing his fingers between hers.

Outside the playhouse, Ethan and Tammy waited with a dozen or so other audience members to greet the cast. Delmar Boulevard was busy with its usual Saturday night traffic, the teenagers and the college kids all rushing to be cultured, to stew among the art with the artists, searching for nuggets of life-knowledge from those who had lived it. The Loop was the center of St. Louis's liberal scene, where boys and girls could wear their grandparent's hats and argue the finer points of socialism while sharing a plate of fresh veggies and humus before dancing to the black music in Chuck Berry's basement. A full mile of different thinkers, alternative music listeners, and independent movie watchers.

The wind picked up, kicking leaves off of trees and sending them down the block. Tammy slid her arms inside Ethan's corduroy jacket and pressed her face against his chest. Bold signs of affection and intimacy were on public display.

They had only spent a handful of nights together. They were moving fast, considering just sixteen days had passed since he offered to buy her a drink. They slept together that night, the first night. Both of them said the obligatory *I don't usually do this*, both also not believing it, not caring either. In the morning they blamed their inability to control lust on being drunk and high. But fuck it, Ethan thought. Here was an attractive woman looking to have a good time with him, why should he deny her that privilege? And he had no one to look after but himself. Still, he felt miserable, and showered for over an hour after Tammy left the duplex. Ethan cried in the shower, cursing his decisions, then he washed his sheets and cleaned the bedroom. The whole morning after, lying in bed with Tammy, he was paranoid Maggie would choose that day to come running back into his arms. Ethan politely kicked her out. "I've got a meeting at the school in an hour. If you don't mind..." He rambled on about IEU's and how important the summer updates were and how he'd be fired if he was late. Tammy didn't care. She left without incident. In fact, she'd had such a good time that she called later that night wanting to make plans for a proper date. And after their proper date, they fucked again, high on cocaine that time, not drunk. He was inside her three more times over the ensuing two nights and one afternoon. Shakespeare was their sixth night together.

It felt both right and wrong, being with Tammy. Each time he repeatedly thought of Maggie and the faces she would make during orgasm. He thought of Maggie's small nipples and the little hair she let herself grow above her clit. But she was gone. For all he knew, at this very moment, her tits could be dangling in front of some other sad fuck's face, making those same faces. He hated Maggie for leaving. So when he was with Tammy, having sex with her, he would finish hard inside to punish Maggie, for quitting and letting things just fall apart.

Ethan put his chin on Tammy's head and pulled her closer inside his jacket. The smell of her hair, her shampoo, her skin, *her* smell, it was all so distinctly different than anything he was used to. His senses had trouble categorizing it; it felt good, but it was unfamiliar. Was it safe or was it a threat? He kissed the top of her head, something he'd never done before. Intimacy did not come easy, yet here he was, so soon after a divorce - Ethan had come to call it a divorce because a simple 'breakup' could not encompass their history, their love, and the subsequent pain he'd been dealt - wrapping his arms around a foreigner. *It fucking feels better than the SHIT I felt before,* his mind would scream. Whenever he had trouble with it he would curse, then suppress his anger, and eventually seek safety deep inside Tammy's web.

He moved to kiss her again, this time to reassure himself, but she pulled away before his lips could touch the top of her head. King Lear had graciously emerged from his dressing quarters, now wearing jeans and a designer T-shirt, to collect praise from the hangers on. The King was a tall man, even without the stage. Ethan made note of the actor's height and age when he bent over to greet Tammy with a hug. Then he kissed her. One mouth pressed up against the other, like old lovers reconnecting. *Who was this old man she knew so well*, he thought.

Ethan found himself coveting her. If there were mixed feelings about how he felt before, they'd suddenly all vanished, like a bubble catching on a blade of grass. She should belong to him, damn it. He needed to have her! And no other man should comfortably press their lips to hers without facing severe consequence, perhaps his fist, perhaps a strong tongue lashing to put the elderly actor in his place. *Get your fucking mouth of her*, he screamed to himself. *I don't care if we met 16 days ago, we have intercourse! And there are marks on my back to prove how much she enjoys it! Stop! Stop touching her arm. Don't you fucking dare touch the small of her back. You're a queer, aren't you? You're an old closeted queer. Stay the fuck away from me and my girl. You don't know what I've been through, old man. This girl is mine and we need each other in ways you only wish you were still young enough to know. Why is she smiling like that? Why did she kiss him back? She kissed him back, right? Or did the whore instigate it, did she invite it? Why am I standing alone in the goddamn cold in U-City? I have half a nerve to leave her here. I could walk back to my car and leave her here with this dusty old man. See if he can fill her like I can! This is how I know she's trash. A real woman, a decent woman, would hold my hand and walk me to her goddamn friends and let them know who she's dancing with. She can put her arms in my jacket but she won't show me off to her celebrity friends? Celebrity!? Fuck HIM! He's doing Community Theater! Is this your life's work, dust? Fucking bitter, saggy chinned old man, your dead wife is watching you grope my girl. How does that make you feel?*

"Ethan," Tammy said, walking back to him, "I want you to meet Richard." The two men shook hands, one confident, the other feigning confidence. Richard was two or three inches taller, but to Ethan it felt like much more. His neck strained from the obtuse

110

angle he had to maintain to look Richard in the eye. "Richard was my acting coach in college." *Ahh, did you lust for him?* "Such an inspiration, as always. You were terrific tonight!"

"Well, it's easy with such an acute audience to play to." Richard was a pro. "You all were right there in it with us, makes my job all the more rewarding." Clearly, he'd done this before.

At some point while the teacher and pupil were telling each other how great they both were, Tammy took Ethan's hand and wrapped his arm around her shoulder. Suddenly, he felt like a man again. Ethan was sure he was now looking eye to eye with Richard, maybe even down on him.

"Listen, Tammy, Ethan, the Players and some friends of ours are going to bonfire and drink scotch. You should join us."

Did he just use bonfire *as a verb?*

"Really?" Tammy was genuine, she was interested. "Where?"

"I don't know really. Somewhere off 40. Not too far out." Richard said. He was looking around for other fans.

"Chesterfield?" she said.

"God, no. No, no, no, no. Close, out that way, but no. Before Maryville. Other side of the interstate."

Ethan did not want to go. He didn't want to share and he was weary of meeting anyone else from Tammy's past so early in their relationship. "Tonight?" he said. He directed it toward Tammy, hoping she would read him correctly.

"Of course tonight," Richard said, interjecting himself. "Come on young man, certainly it's not too late for you. It's a wrap party of sorts. A celebration of our final night with Lord Shakespeare. What do you say?"

Ethan stared at Tammy, waiting for her to do the right thing, but she paid no attention. She didn't even look his way.

"I say, Fuck Yes." Tammy was excited. Her mind was made up. "Wait, Michael won't be there will he?"

This is exactly what I'm talking about. Who the fuck is Michael?

"No, I think not. You've heard what happened to him, haven't you..." Richard kept talking but Ethan tuned the rest out. His ears were numb and he stood dumbstruck with a half assed stupid smile plastered on his face. He didn't have the courage to stand up to King Lear and deny his invitation.

Ethan was embarrassed and angry at the party. The temperature dropped noticeably and he fought off shivers within his bones. Tammy and he arrived together, but that was all. While she reconnected with old friends, he drank. The scotch tasted like piss in his mouth but he drank it anyway. He loathed scotch, always had. The lone redeeming quality to the party was the fire, and even that was a challenge to enjoy. People wanted to know him and how he fit into their circle. They wanted to small talk. All Ethan wanted was to get piss drunk and fuck Tammy. He also wanted to leave her there, cut her, shock her. If he picked up a bottle on the way home he could throw on a record and enjoy what was left of the weekend. Maybe spend Sunday cleaning and watching those Looney Tune DVD's Winslow had given him for Christmas. Lord knows the bathtub needed scrubbing, something he'd been avoiding for six weeks. Then again, maybe not. Maybe he should just relax and save some energy. Those fucking kids were going to need him on Monday morning.

EXPOSITION

There is a moment, a spark that ignites, when things finally click inside the human brain. When all the information comes together at once, and the answer is embarrassingly clear, that is when the puzzle is complete. It's as if someone flipped the switch inside the mind and all of the lights came on at once, illuminating everything, all of the dark corners, all of the unanswered and unclear questions: the Light Bulb Moment. The Light Bulb Moment is precisely why Ethan became a teacher. The joy he took in watching child after child discover a new chunk of knowledge, watching them flip the switch and light up, that joy was incalculable. It was life's natural euphoria, produced solely by positive human connection.

And it would happen literally in an instant. Dark to Light. The algebra problem is a foreign language, like nothing spoken before, utterly mysterious. Then, it clicks! X has value! The muscles in the tiny foreheads of the young students would collectively jolt toward the sky, their spines became erect, and a smile, usually a sheepish smile, would gather at the corners of their mouths.

Ethan lived for this moment. No matter how much shit was piled onto a day, no matter the situation at home, no matter the authoritative warnings handed down by Principal Fenske, no matter the unexpected home repairs or the 'late payment' notice, no matter the bitter lovers' quarrel or the parking ticket, no matter how much the cloud rained down upon him in a single day, it could all be erased when the lights were turned on.

The Light Bulb Moment had power.

It cut through the bullshit and brought two people face to face, helping one another in a special way they'd carry with them for a lifetime. Two or three decades later, the young student would recall his Light Bulb Moment, he would thank his teacher for helping him find the light switch, and then wonder where the teacher was now, hoping he was living out his days in peace.

Ethan thought of Mr. Rathner often, about where he was in life, and whether or not he was a happy man, if he was still teaching, still flipping switches. Rathner was the greatest, an inspiration. He gave the gift of light to Ethan, so Ethan could in turn pass it down to others.

EXPOSITION

Man Y and woman X meet in a social setting. They have drinks, they converse, and generally enjoy each other's company. Y and X decide on a formal dinner, a date. It goes well, and everything ends in smiles and happy feelings. Man Y enjoys woman X and after several months of courting they decide to become a committed team, an official couple, off limits to the rest of society. Their love grows, and they form strong bonds which are anchored in trust and emotional dependability. Their commitment is proven honorable for a lengthy period of time, one that feels comfortable to both the couple, and their friends and family. Eventually, vows are agreed to be spoken, and formerly separate families are legally fused together as one, for all of eternity.

Y loves X, and together they turn wood and nails and fabric and furniture and plates and plaster and paint, into a lovely and comforting home, a place to raise a family. Years pass. Their love changes, but it continues to grow and evolve into its own indescribable entity. Then, rather unfortunately, Man Y begins to bring the office home with him. The office is full of stress. Life has become difficult for Y and X. Woman X begins to feel inadequate. She fears she can no longer capture Y's attention. Y no longer looks at X as he did years ago, as he did when they first met in the social setting over drinks and conversation. Their love changes.

Woman X feels that an addition might bring Man Y's attention back into their home. X feels that a baby may just be an excellent solution. A child is born! Y is a father! He is happy again! X is a mother and she is happy again! She is happy her plan is working!

Man Y and Woman X and Baby Jacob spend countless hours together, in the park, in their home, with grandparents, at the Zoo, watching movies on the couch, tossing the ball around the yard. Baby Jacob starts to grow. But when Baby Jacob goes to school, he has problems learning. Baby Jacob is violent with other children and screams with sadistic authority at his teachers. Baby Jacob also cries, constantly. Life had become difficult again for Y and X.

Woman X takes Baby Jacob to his pediatrician. After multiple tests, and second and third opinions, Baby Jacob is diagnosed with Bi-Polar Disorder. Man Y feels inferior and responsible for his son's deficiency. Woman X feels inferior and responsible for her son's deficiency. Y and X also blame each other. New stress is brought into the relationship. Their love changes yet again. Dialogue between Y and X is rare, and aggressive behavior becomes a regular occurrence due to their lack of communication.

Man Y feels he has no options. He questions his love for X and wonders if she has any love left for him. No one is happy, and Man Y knows it's foolish to continue prolonging the inevitable. Y leaves the home and leaves X and leaves Baby Jacob. Woman X signs divorce papers. The trust and the bond and the love are all shattered. Only photographs and stories remain as proof that they were once happy people.

Man Y and Woman X meet in a social setting. Baby Jacob is a product of their failed attempt at love.

EXPOSITION

On the back wall just below a row of windows in Principal Fenske's office at Park View Elementary, there is a bookshelf. The bookshelf is 36 inches high and stretches the length of the office, a custom job. One section on the bottom shelf is filled with large, white, three-ring binders, each of them containing a personalized, yellow medical dispensation form. These are the parental release forms, and they empower Park View Elementary to administer prescription drugs to students in need of timely medication. They also contain important information for students who happen to be traveling with prescription medication. For instance: When a child from a separated (divorce or born out of wedlock) or blended (one or both parents have remarried) family is switching households mid-week due to court mandated custody, the student must check-in his or her prescriptions with their assigned teacher. At the end of the day, when the student moves from mothers house to fathers, or vice versa, the medication is placed in the hands of the student at the moment the parent arrives to pick them up after school. Each three ring binder contains permission, information about the student's condition, and directions for administration.

It is not an unflawed system, but it works. It works primarily because of the upper middle class school district Park View Elementary happens to geographically fall into, but also because of the general concern and honesty by the parents, the students, and the faculty. There are many tests done and background checks performed on prospective teachers before they are granted such great responsibility. FBI criminal background checks, drug checks, relevant personal medical history, as well as state-required mental health evaluations, are all just part of the strenuous protocol. The accredited college degrees, the tests, the interviews, they are all designed to weed out unqualified and 'at risk' teachers. All in all, the system works. It works because it has to. The students need medication to maintain focus, to learn, and to excel. The parents trust the administrators, the administrators trust the teachers. And it is all designed to protect the students.

OCTOBER 6

"Look, Jake, you can't beat yourself up," Ethan said leaning in, trying to persuade the kid to stay positive. "Dividing fractions is a tough thing to wrap your head around. If it wasn't, I'd be out of a job. You wanna know a secret?"

Jacob didn't respond. He was locked out and all he could manage were physical manifestations of frustration. With one hand, he tugged repeatedly at a chunk of hair, his head bobbing like a yo-yo, with the other, he forced the pink eraser on the butt of his pencil into his forehead. It was a subconscious attempt to jam the answer past his skull, directly into his brain.

"Jake, stop that, bubba," Ethan said as he took the pencil out of the boy's hand and set it down on his notebook. "You're gonna slip and drive that thing into your eye. And I'm not qualified to clean up that kind of mess."

The boy laughed but he was still frustrated, it didn't click, he wasn't even sure he wanted it to anymore. He just wanted it to be over. When the kids tuned out, they often deployed distraction tactics. They'd talk about something in the room, or ask meaningless personal questions, anything to divert attention. Sometimes nature would suddenly call. Sometimes they'd just giggle in hopes that their goddamn cuteness would buy them a ticket out of town, away from the problem. Jake was at that point, ready to switch gears and abandon fractions for distracting moments of life. He was stuck in the dark with a mathematical problem that had no apparent solution.

This was Ethan's job: to show patience where parents couldn't, to provide the extra push, while still holding on to the students hand.

"Jake, answer me," Ethan said, making sure to capture his attention. "You wanna know a secret? It's a good one, I promise."

Jake finally nodded.

"Your mom doesn't know how to divide fractions either." He said the words like he'd just invented the world's first nuclear weapon. "And you know what else? When I'm done with you, you're gonna be just a little bit smarter than she is."

Jake liked the way that sounded, his eyebrows came together at an angle.

Ethan, seeing an opening, pressed on. "Now, tell me what you think one divided by half is."

"Point five. No! Half?" Jake was trying, he was desperate, but at least he was trying.

"Okay, that's not the right answer. But that's okay." Ethan got up from the student desk he was sitting in and walked toward his own desk at the front of the room. "So, I tell you what, I'm gonna give you a trick to figure it out. Okay?"

Ethan opened the bottom drawer, but he was covert about it, he needed Jake to know that this trick, this special solution, was not for all the students, only for the special ones. There was a secret stash in the bottom drawer, a food stash, and Ethan walked back to Jake shaking a box of Graham Crackers. "The Secret Weapon," said Ethan as he pulled a long cracker from the box.

Jake looked excitedly at his teacher. Ethan stepped into character; he was like every bad impression of Sherlock Holms rolled into one, all he needed was the pipe. "What is this?" he asked.

"A Graham Cracker."

"Right you are, my dear boy, right you are. But it is also more than that. It is also the number ONE. Do you understand, my dear boy? This cracker is a cracker but it is also the number one." Ethan showed the cracker in his left hand, and used his index finger of his right hand at the number one, alternating them in front of Jake's eyes. "Now, my dear boy," he presented the cracker, "if we divide this number one in half…" Ethan snapped the cracker directly down its middle seam. "If we divide one in half we get?"

"TWO!" Jake shouted.

"Two! That is correct, my dear boy, two indeed. Elementary, Watson." Ethan took a bite out of one half and tossed the other half to Jake. Then, he pulled out two more whole crackers from the box. "Two divided by half is what?"

"Four!"

It was Jacob's light bulb moment.

Ethan smashed the crackers together in celebration, sending hundreds of crumbs to the floor. Then, like a jubilant fan, he started cheering and running through the rows of desks, arms waving in the air. His voice took on the persona of an announcer, "The crowd goes wild! I cannot believe what I just saw. Jacob Kirby… knows… how… to… divide… by Fractions!" Cupping his hands over his mouth, he cheered again on his way back up the aisle. Ethan gave the kid a high-five, and his eyes were lit with joy.

122

"That's my man," Ethan said, out of breath and falling down into his chair. "Now, run to the bathroom and grab some paper towels so we can clean this mess up. I don't want Fenske yelling at me. I'll blame you. I'll tell her you made me do it. You held me hostage and said if I didn't give you an 'A' you'd smash my brains like you did those cookies."

They both laughed and then Jake walked out for the bathroom, leaving Ethan alone in his classroom. Ethan scratched the surface of his scalp, feeling dead skin and dirt collect beneath his fingernails. It grossed him out but there was some fun in it. And it felt good, like all the hair follicles were awake at once and dancing.

His attention drifted toward the long row of windows on the far wall and out beyond. The sun was falling out of sight over the horizon, like a cruise ship sailing off into the ocean. The tall parking lot street lamps flickered until they were warm and shining brightly. Just past the parking lot there was a large open field where the students would gather for recess and home soccer games. It was quiet in the classroom, but questions of metaphysics were singing loudly inside the teacher's head. Images of his own schooldays were floating past his mind's eye, one after another, unattached to anything other than a peculiar feeling, an emotion, one that was tough to pin down and identify. A cliché was as close as he could get: A simpler time. A time that wasn't entirely long ago, just an instant in the universal scheme, but on a teacher's timeline, half a life had past, maybe his entire life had passed, and he missed it, missed everything. How was it possible, he thought, that these youthful images could be so real, so readily available in the cortex, but also completely elusive, as if merely recalling one would cause it to fade away into nothingness?

From the window he looked out onto the dark empty field and saw himself, a nine-year-old boy flying the kite he'd made in art class, sprinting through the grass, begging the wind to catch up with him and lift his hand-made toy into the sky. He saw fourteen-year-old Ethan dribble the soccer ball with the tips of his toes, dodging players and making incredibly athletic moves. He shoots, and the ball sails into the back of the net. A goal! But against whom? Where was the team in celebration? Where was the defense or the goalie or anyone or anything? Did this even happen? Truth be told, Ethan hated soccer. Sure he played as a kid, but not for the love of the sport, he played to be social and make friends. But he played, so surely this memory must've been real. Red Umbros, he remembered those. Red and white socks. He ran track in school, wore the school colors there too, did the long jump into a pit of wretched sand. There was a Blue Ribbon somewhere in his grandparents' house, wasn't there? Hanging on the corner of the mirror. Or was it white? Was it a White Ribbon, for participation? It didn't rain in these memories. Never once. Was weather never a factor in his past? Did it only rain in the present? Surely these events all happened! But where is the documentation, the proof!? Why wasn't any of this recorded anywhere? First kiss, second grade, in the hallway near the science lab. Bell rings. *Hide that bad grade, no wait, throw it away.* No evidence, nothing recorded. There is grandma, waiting at the door, she was never late picking him up from school. *Hug her.* Her hug felt like home, the way a puppy must feel when a boy lifts if from its box inside the pet store. Grandma felt warm and safe and free from anything that resembled harm. It felt like a mother. He hated mothers! *Fuck mothers, they're an urban legend.* The field. The goalpost. It was summer in the cortex, always summer and never any rain inside the cortex. *Did any of this ever even happen?* Did he live this life at all?

"I'm headed home." Principal Fenske's voice nearly shocked Ethan's heart into an attack. She had knocked, after she'd already opened the door and poked her head into his room. "I've got Jacob Kirby's medication here," she said, as she set it on the

124

nearest desk. "Make sure Lind Kirby signs off on it, please." She placed a thick three-ring binder next to the medicine, opened it to the autograph page, and turned to leave. "IEU's updates are two weeks away. You're going to be ready, right?" It was a command, not a question.

Ethan nodded.

"Kill the lights when you leave, this place is hemorrhaging money. Good night." She left and closed the door, it clicked when it shut completely.

The old chair made its loud noise when he got up and walked toward the gifts Fenske had just brought him. Pills. Adderal PX. An AD(H)D prescription at 400 milligrams which was used to treat Jake's bipolar disorder. The drug seemed to blend well with his chemical makeup, causing extended periods of focus and higher scholastic production. Another added benefit: his outbursts were completely absent during school days. Those happy little pills were smiling up at Ethan, offering similar peace.

He took off the lid and placed six pills inside the left breast pocket of his oxford shirt. For a moment he hesitated, looked over his shoulder and out the windowpane of the door, then he removed one more pill and held it in his hand until it was moist from palm sweat. Ethan popped the lid back on and walked to his desk just as Jake reentered with paper towels. Ethan watched as the kid cleaned the mess of a million Graham Crackers off the floor.

OCTOBER 6

The felt at Nick's Pub was a vibrant cardinal red, and the edges were pulled tight to the corners of the table, no scuffs or beer stains either. Management autographed a sign that read "NO drinks near the table!" which helped keep things clean. Both of the tables were on the second floor where it was quieter and less rowdy than the ground level. The ground level, the first floor, was for underage students and binge drinking. It was for drunkenly singing the chorus to whatever twenty or thirty-year-old pop song was playing from the jukebox, or on Thursdays, from the hired one man cover band. Adults ventured upstairs, for billiards and conversation, and the narrow, rickety staircase helped keep most of the intoxicated away. However, it wasn't uncommon to find young lovers hiding in a corner up on the second floor, with one hand inside a blouse and the other on a pint of Guinness. All in all, it was a nice spot for old friends, brothers-in-law, to shoot a game of pool.

"So this punk," Winslow said, increasing his volume as the story progressed. "Who wouldn't have a pot to piss in if it weren't for nepotism, says he 'aint feelin' it,' and that maybe he needed a producer who was a bit more 'in touch', someone who could 'feel' him." Winslow used quotation fingers too, selling his story as hard as he could.

Ethan wasn't listening. He had heard all the words, and could probably repeat them verbatim, but he most certainly was not listening. He drew the stick back and then shot it forward, launching the white ball through the triangle, dropping the fourteen, and giving Ethan permission to move behind the cue again to line up the next stripe.

"In touch. *In touch*," Winslow said it the second time with disgust as it came off his tongue and past his teeth. "The punk has balls, I'll give him that much. Anyway, so I mic into the studio and say, 'How long have you been around, son?' And he looks at me all confused and doesn't know what to say."

Ethan dropped the fifteen ball, giving Winslow more time to talk.

"So I ask him again, 'How long you been around, huh? And how long you think you're gonna last? Because I've been doin' this long before your conception, and I'm still here.' The little punk froze, right there on the spot, stopped talkin' all together. 'Show some respect, *Feel That*' I told him. I don't think he thought the old man had it in him."

Ethan sunk two more striped balls.

"Jesus, are you gonna let me shoot here, brother?"

Ethan struck the nine-ball with a light touch, giving it just enough to tumble into the side pocket. The eleven was the last stripe on the table, and a clean shot would have nailed it, but he missed a little left, and it rattled the corners. Ethan backed off the table and moved to befriend his beer.

"You alright tonight? Seem a little..." *Low, down, off, depressed, miserable to fucking be around.* Winslow just let the sentence trail away.

Ethan shrugged off the question. No big deal. Nothing to worry about.

He was low. And with good reason. The past few months had been full of peaks and valleys, but all the peaks seemed to be hidden somewhere deep within a very dark and grim valley. Life was dealing body blows and breaking ribs. The failed engagement left him only memories of a happy home and a laughing, smiling Maggie. Their love was so thick it couldn't crack, but it did. It cracked all the way through, separating them. Like the unsinkable Titanic, an iceberg ripped open their gut, and they sunk. Only there were no survivors. And there was still that goddamned image, that one frame he couldn't edit out, which stuck him like a cattle prod every time he closed his eyes. The red paint flowing from her thighs and down the rusted drain.

It seemed as if there was only one remedy to neutralize that emotional poison: Chemicals. Any combination, any dosage, any label. So long as it had a brash and sweeping effect to disengage the mind from its constant negative thought process, it would work, it would be the drug of choice. Whatever was nearest and strongest, he would use.

"Are you sure? You sure you're okay?" Winslow asked again.

With a slow turn of his head, Ethan studied his brother-in-law's face, his tiny pores, his odd frame and bone structure, his forehead growing as his hairline withered. It was only a matter of time, he figured, before he would start shaving his head like every other self-conscious, balding young American male. For a brief moment, Ethan considered playing that game of judgment on

Winslow, the father to his unborn nephew, but ultimately he decided against it. He felt sorry enough for him and his plight. The study continued as he examined Winslow's large eyeballs, wide and alert, like a rabbit. He was a bunny, Ethan decided, a small bunny with wide eyes, excited to be alive and bouncing on his white puffy tail, but also terrified of everything. Whether it was his own shadow, or a cold breeze ruffling his fur, it petrified him. He was nothing more than a house rabbit, waiting to be scolded or caressed, or to have a carrot shoved in between the bars of his tiny cage. A pet. What a pitiful existence, Ethan thought, what a shit way to move through life. *No*, he said to himself, still staring at Winslow, *I'll spare him the game, he's suffered enough*.

"What did it feel like?" Ethan asked.

All the concern fell from Winslow's face and was instantly replaced with curiosity. "What did what feel like?"

"When you found out. About your son."

"Ethan…" Winslow put his cue aside and sat on his stool. Nonverbally, he was submitting, waving the white flag before the battle had even begun. "Come on, I don't wanna do this."

"I do."

Winslow laughed. There was nothing else he could think to do, so he laughed.

"I want to know what I didn't get to feel," Ethan said, calm as a lake on a humid summer day with a green sky rolling above, moments before the downpour.

"You're drunk," Winslow laughed and smiled, so nervous he could shit himself.

"Don't be an asshole, Winslow."

"Hey, come on now."

"I'm asking a question and I want an answer. The way things are looking, I'm not going to get to know firsthand. I want you to tell me about it. Tell me what I didn't get to feel."

"Are you drunk? How many is that for you, brother?" Winslow's voice got higher, like a soprano. "That's why I don't do that shit anymore, the drinkin'. Start talkin' about shit, not even knowing what you're sayin'."

During the course of their conversation, two men – young enough to still be fuck ups but too old to be wearing oversized polo shirts and flat billed hats with stickers still on them – made their way up the flimsy staircase, and rested their backs against the bar. The skinny one barked at Ethan and Winslow, "You done shootin'?" He talked tough, wanted to be tough, wanted to be something else, or someone else.

"There are still balls on the table aren't there?" Ethan shouted back without so much as flinching to look in their direction.

"You gonna play or just keep talkin'?"

Ethan snapped and turned toward them as he stood up from his stool. "Shut up and leave my friend and I alone. We're conversing. Do you understand that?"

Winslow leaped forward and stood between Ethan and the two wiggers, who were both standing tall with their chests puffed out. "I'm sorry, guys! Don't listen to him," Winslow said. "We're almost done and then you guys got next." The two men turned around, mumbling useless rhetoric to each other. Winslow was jumpy but he had successfully diffused the situation.

Once he was sure they wouldn't retaliate with broken bottles and brass knuckles, Winslow stood toe-to-toe with Ethan, challenging him but saying nothing, waiting for an explanation. There was a smirk on Ethan's face, not the wide grin variety, small rather, barely noticeable, but it was clear that the muscles in his face were prideful and excited. Ethan set his glass on a coaster and then, in a bizarre expression of affection, pulled Winslow into his chest and swallowed him with an aggressive hug. It was so genuine it felt phony. Neither man spoke. Finally, Ethan released his grip and took Winslow by the shoulders, admiring him like a cheap plastic bowling trophy. Moving his hands up from the shoulders and then to the base of Winslow's skull, where the head rests on the neck, Ethan pulled him in again, pressing his lips against Winslow's cheek, kissing him. And again, he kissed Winslow a second time, mouth to whiskers. Ethan leaned back, putting a small amount of distance between them, and smiled at his brother-in-law.

"I've gotta piss. Rack 'em up." And with that, Ethan left Winslow stunned, and turned the corner toward the men's room.

Nick's Pub's upstairs pisser was small enough for a fat person to press both arms against the wall simultaneously, without lifting either wrist more than a few inches from their waist, yet both a urinal and a toilet were compressed inside the tiny hole. Ethan had to lock the deadbolt and the door knob, and give a quick look around the corners of the ceiling for any possible security cameras, before he felt secure and alone. Paranoia had begun to dictate Ethan's actions. Standing over the toilet, one leg on each side of the bowl, he wiped the tank cover with his forearm and elbow to sanitize his workspace. From his left breast pocket he removed two of Jacob Kirby's pills and set them center stage across the toilet tank lid. He then took his cell from his pant pocket, and with the delicate precision of an apothecary, who would grind drug with mortar and pestle, crushed the Adderall into dust with the butt of his cellular phone. Leaning forward, Ethan pressed the side of his face against the porcelain lid and pulled the Speed into his nose. He quickly gathered the remainder with the sides of his hands and pulled that into the other nostril.

Ethan pushed out a scream, a cheer really, that seemed to already be waiting in the bottom of his throat. He pounded the wall until it stung his hand, as if it were his teammates, celebrating the win with a row of high-five's. Ethan looked around the bathroom again for cameras, and when he saw none, he gave the finger to various points in the room in case the eyes that may be watching were very well hidden. There was no mirror to check in with, probably for the better, because he may have smashed it to prove his strength and superiority, so he washed his hands and splashed his face, and flushed the toilet to fool anyone waiting on the other side of the door.

Suddenly the music coming from the band downstairs was alive. He could feel the beat rising through the floorboards, sending an electric current through his feet and up the back of his legs. The music was a spark, it gave him life. Wherever he moved, he left a colorful trail of energy behind him.

At the tables, Winslow was still on edge. Ethan slapped him on the shoulder and assured him that everything was going to be okay. Then he turned to the wiggers, with the stickers on their hats and oversized clothing. "You two want the table?" Ethan shouted across the bar at the two men. "Let's play for it. Twenty bucks a game? Fifty? What do you say?"

Winslow abruptly stood up, attempting to interject, but Ethan raised his arm, like Moses commanding the Red Sea, and stopped him where he stood. "Don't screw this up, my Brother," Ethan said with a sinister smile. "We've got a college fund to start saving for."

OCTOBER 11

Deep in the trenches of desire, Ethan had always longed to smash his guitar. Even as a child, taking lessons in the church basement from the kid who only played Christmas and Easter mass, there was a hunger for that Rock and Roll moment where he could grip its neck and swing it like an ax, full force into another object. He wanted to *know* Pete Townshend or Paul Simonon, to feel that rush of destruction, the total dominance of man over machine, and give a giant middle finger to his instrument, to his art, to the whole goddamn world. He didn't need a stage, or even an audience to impress, all he wanted was the reckless abandon, the adrenaline to course through him as the wood splintered and the strings broke free in his hands. And if he was lucky, perhaps if his grip was tight enough, the steel of the High E string could tear through some softer portion of flesh, maybe between his fingers, draw some blood and leave a scar, a reminder of the moment he allowed caution to get pissed on in the wind. What a blessing, he thought, to forego consequence and live in the moment, the rush.

Why not now? The words seemed to float out of his mind and across his living room. *You should stand up and do it.* It was scrolling commentary, and he watched the big letters take shape, and form the goading command right before his eyes.

The black case was sitting innocently in the corner, next to his record player, like a lobster in a tank not knowing it was about to be boiled. He could do it, he thought. He could remove the guitar and let its body explode against the wall or against the television or against the tile on the edge of the kitchen counter. *Why not?*

Instead he poured a half glass of wine and re-corked the bottle. As he drank, he held the wine over his tongue for a long moment, trying to discern its various qualities, but it was useless. His pallet was about as accurate as a blind man in a shooting range. Nevertheless, he drank it, and it made him feel good because it made him drunk. Just as the man with no sight relished in the joy of pulling the trigger, giving fuckall to what the bullet might hit, Ethan loved the drunk, and he couldn't care how the rain, or soil, effected the grape's growing season.

So he sat on the couch, a little high and half drunk, arms crossed, feet flat on the floor, staring at the black guitar case in the corner of the living room. There was a time when it used to be fun to play, when there was an exchange of life and love between Ethan and that old guitar. It used to be, playing would recharge his soul. And Maggie had no choice but to give into him completely, she was utterly lost in his talent. Her eyes would fixate on his fingers, and her body would melt into the chair, or the floor, or whatever structure happened to be supporting her. She would smile at him with pride, with desire.

The first time she heard him play she kissed him. They were strangers then. Maggie was in her robe and flip flops, walking to her dorm room from the community showers on Fusz Hall's fifth floor. The door was closed but not all the way, a good three or six inch crack still remained. Ethan wanted people to hear him play. Maggie, still wet from the shower, followed the sound - every asshole in college could strum an acoustic guitar but this was different, she thought, she heard plucking and picking, mixed with energy and sadness, and the song was original, not some shitty, heartless cover (this is what stood out to her, what altered her path) - she followed the sound past the showers to room 505, and pushed the cracked door open fully. Unable to stop herself, she walked right into the room, uninvited and unnoticed, and sat down on one of the mattresses. There were two beds, one belonging to Ethan, the other, his roommate, and Ethan was in a chair in the center of the room between the beds. He was facing the window, singing occasionally, but mostly just playing the instrument, and playing it so damn beautifully that he managed to pull a gorgeous freshman girl, fully naked beneath her robe, into his room and onto his bed. The whole scene was like something ripped from a movie. It's the reason every boy picks up a guitar in the first place. And while he didn't know she was there in the room with him (his back was toward her), he most certainly was playing for an audience. After all, he had left the door open.

"Play another," she said when he finished. He jumped, startled, first that he wasn't alone, second that she was nearly naked. He acted bashful, embarrassed to have *any*one hear him play. Then Ethan played another song, this time turning the chair to face her, to sing to her, and when he finished he saw that her eyes were damp. She got off his bed, kissed him on the cheek, and told him how talented she thought he was.

And that was it, the beginning of their love, the moment that started it all. For years Ethan and Maggie took great pleasure in recounting that story, embellishing minor details, while poking fun at one another throughout – *He was so sad playing in there, I felt bad for him / Oh she's lying, the song made her so hot, she couldn't help but take off her clothes before coming into my room, in fact, I think it was my robe she was wearing.* – But they were always touching and smiling upon the story's completion.

Not once from that day forward did he pick up the guitar without thinking of that kiss, and the softness of her lips, they way she took her time, making sure to hold her face near his as long as the moment would allow. It felt like an eternity, like he could live in that moment forever, until he was old and wrinkled. She had long blonde hair then, he remembered, and she'd thrown it up in a sloppy pony tail for the shower. And the pink towel, so downy and thick against the skin of his upper arm. Maggie's face was clear and shiny, glowing. But she was still a mystery, an angel appearing in his room, summoned by his song. He didn't even know her name.

It took time to develop and understand the feelings that had surfaced that night inside his dorm room. Maggie went back home for summer vacation, Ethan moved into the duplex. But when August came and classes resumed, they found each other in a lecture hall seated just several rows apart. She turned her head, her eyes met his.

Two nights later, she was eating dinner inside the Tower Grove Park duplex, with Ethan and Rachel and Winslow.

That same old guitar, spitting out images of that awful memory, was locked inside its black case and staring at Ethan from across the room. There was blood trapped in that case, an empty promise, a lie. He swallowed the rest of the wine, quickly this time, and closed his eyes. His head was far too heavy to support so it fell to one side.

•

When he came to the music was loud and Tammy was working her hips and spine, the way a Slinky walks down stairs, slow and snake-like, with all the pieces working together. Her arms were moving in the opposite direction, walking upwards, lifting that thick blanket of red hair, and exposing the line of her neck. She turned profile and stared down at Ethan from the corner of her eye.

Still drunk and dazed, Ethan sat up. For almost a full minute he was confused, like waking suddenly in the middle of the night inside a strange house and needing to piece the room together before the puzzle could make any sense. But he wasn't at all scared or bitter. He just watched her dance. And with each beat of the drum, he watched his wine glass vibrate across the glass-topped wooden coffee table, and then he saw the record spinning, and then his guitar case. And then it was clear that he'd fallen asleep and Tammy had let herself in.

"The door was unlocked. I hope you don't mind," Tammy said over the pounding speakers.

She crossed the room with a slow catwalk, her toes attempting to contact the ground in correlation to the music. With the coffee table and their clothing still separating them, Tammy turned her back toward Ethan and slipped out of her jeans. She wore a thong perfectly. Turning back to face him, she threw her thigh into the air and lifted herself on top of the coffee table, up onto her stage, and impressively, in the same motion, she removed her t-shirt. But rather than look at her chest, Ethan's eyes went down to the base of the coffee table, thinking how pissed off he'd be if she broke it. He'd rescued it from the streets so many years ago, and carried it on his back for miles, back to the duplex. It was one of a kind, it was irreplaceable.

With her legs posted wide and stiff, she looked like an inverted Y towering over him. Then, she bent over at the waist, her tits at war with her bra for freedom, and grabbed the wine

137

bottle. "I am high on mushrooms right now and I want to fuck you," she said, full of sex. It needed to be released. Tammy ripped the cork out with her teeth, blew it to the floor, and sucked down several mouthfuls of red wine. She glared down on him again, this time with a sadistic smile on her face, took one more drink, and stepped off the table. Leaning over him, her forehead touching his forehead, her red mane draping and surrounding his entire skull, she wrapped her legs around his waist, and lifted his chest into hers. She opened her mouth, pressed it to his, and transferred the last of the wine into him. They finished with wet lips and soft tongues pressing together.

Ethan's clothes came off quickly somewhere between the couch and the foot of the bed. The music was thumping loudly, louder than before, and now they were part of the song. Blood was pulsating to the beat, humping and sweating, and the music enhanced every stroke, every squeeze, every moan. Ethan lost his finger in the line where her legs connected. He could feel her moisture and he spread it across her bare skin. She moaned and tossed her head back, exposing a naked ear lobe.

"Everything is purple," she said as he bit her neck. "All I see is purple. It's so wonderful."

Tammy's hands were strong and dry, like a manual laborer, and they dug into his back for support. Her hands were a stark contrast from Maggie's.

Maggie was soft and delicate. Maggie didn't kiss like this and she was gent –

Ethan slammed his eyes lids tight, closing the door and shoving Maggie out of his consciousness. He wanted to focus on Tammy, on something real and tangible, so he took her in in sections: her chest was flush, her nipples, full and sensitive, the round, brown freckle above her right breast. He kissed the freckle.

The music slowed as they finished. She screamed a guttural, primordial scream, and it was low and it gave him permission to fill her. Her leg trembled. No one spoke a word, just heavy breathing.

And then it set in. Anger and guilt tore through Ethan's body. He cringed at her every move. The soft rising and falling of her chest made him want to reach over and smother her, gut her even. The joints in his fingers and toes were lodged with hatred and self-loathing. Who was this whore he let in his bed? He promised himself he'd stop, that he'd deny Tammy the right to his body, the right to grind him and cum on him. Somehow he thought it would honor his last relationship, and somewhere he thought, he hoped, Maggie was still coming back.

But now…now, *FUCK IT*. Now, there was a whore with her head on his wife's pillow, and she was still moaning and shaking with delight. If he could bring himself to touch her he might kill her. *What a stupid girl*, he said to himself, *what stupid things she said during intercourse, and what a whore she was to come into my house higher than a fucking NASA rocket and expect me to give her my soul.* He curled into a ball on the furthest edge of the bed. *Look at you. You're the whore, not her. A stupid, cheap whore. You're pathetic, you know that? What would she think of you now? Would she even know you? I'm so sorry, Mags. I am so sorry. I never should have touched her, not the first time, not now. I never should have talked to her or looked at her. But you left me, you took my life, and left me with nothing. I fucked her hoping I could find you, somewhere inside of her, inside me. I don't know where to turn. The kids at school don't help anymore and Rachel is fucking pregnant, she's pregnant with our baby! She took our kid from us. And all I have is this shit, this fucking misery and darkness eating away at the lining of my stomach like a cancer. But it's worse than cancer, more debilitating than anything else on earth. It grows and burns away my insides, laughing at me all the while, telling me how fucking useless this whole life is, that it's all meaningless. And I believe it! I truly do!*

139

When you left and you put your ring on our bed I knew nothing mattered. It was all fleeting. And now all I can do to escape, all I can do to find a moment of nothing, not joy, but not this gut burning pain either, all I can do to reach that moment of nothing is-

"I can't move," Tammy said, interrupting his thought. "It was so good. I'm not going to clean off."

Ethan wanted to scream. He wanted to scare her and then empty her of any life, to remove her completely from existence. If she was gone, then there would be no proof that this mistake ever happened. Maggie would be home soon, he was sure of it. And Tammy had to go. He had to remove her quickly: wash the sheets, make sure none of her red hairs were buried between pillows, and then shower. He wanted nothing more than to shower her off of his body. The thought of her juice and sweat seeping through his pores made him want to vomit.

For no explicable reason, he disobeyed his every thought and desire, and rolled to her, wrapping an arm around her body and cupping her breast in his hand. Ethan was so full of detestation toward himself, he could only think in terms of punishment. *Live with this new body, smell the shit you've stepped in.*

He kissed her shoulder. There was nothing left. The chemistry between them was lost inside her and on the sheets. Another stain on the mattress.

"I bet you're a good teacher. I bet those kids love you," she said. "You're so sweet."

Ethan fought the urge to take her throat in his hands.

•

In the bathroom he held a bottle of seventy percent solution isopropyl alcohol up to his nose and inhaled deeply a dozen times. His shoulders dropped, his brow relaxed. The

140

shower water was hot and it nearly burned his skin. He scrubbed his penis and chest and rubbed his mouth and lips vigorously. When he came out of the bathroom, Tammy was sound asleep. Most of the covers were bunched up in a ball on the floor, and she was sprawled out naked across the bed. Ethan covered her and went into the living room. The record player was skipping so he turned it off. He sat on the couch, staring at the black guitar case, until he fell asleep.

OCTOBER 18

"Six - four," Lind Kirby said while wiping sweat off his brow with his wrist band. "Check it." He tossed the ball to Russ. Russ nodded over both shoulders to ready the Shirts for defense before he passed it back to Lind.

There was a ball screen to Russ's right, so Lind jabbed one way before cutting back and rubbing Russ off on the man who set the pick. Lind dribbled to open space and made a smooth bounce pass to the screener, who was rolling down the lane after the pick. He was wide open, the pick and roll worked to perfection. The man rolling caught the pass in transition and turned to score. And he would have, but he was forty six years old and his awkward feet struggled to support his lumpy body. By the time he was ready to shoot, he'd dribbled twice and ended up below the rim and in the air. He threw up an ugly shot and it clanked against the bottom of the basket. Ethan, playing for the shirts, grabbed the rebound.

"Come on! You gotta have those," Lind said loudly in disgust. "I can't get it to you any better than that, shithead. Gotta have those."

"He's on *your* team, *shithead*." Ethan's quick, strong retort surprised everybody on the court, but he remained firm, with a certain boldness in his step. He dribbled the ball hard against the floor several times, glaring at Lind, challenging him to respond. With half the guys distracted, looking at Lind, Ethan made a move at the top of the key, he went left, beating his defender, and driving for the lane. Lind left his own man to stop the penetration, but he was late, so he reached for the ball, swinging his arm like a windmill, and striking Ethan just above the wrist.

"Foul," Ethan said, almost in a whisper, as the ball came loose.

"FOUL?!" shouted Lind. "Keep dreaming, teach."

Ethan's eyes flared as he stuck his chest out, restraining himself from marching over to Lind and ripping his eyes out of their sockets. He spoke instead. "You ripped my arm off!"

"Hey man, don't come in weak. I got your finger, maybe, and the hand is part of the ball. You can't come in weak, right coach?" Lind dropped the ball at Russ's feet again. "Check it up."

"You're an asshole, you know that? Cop or not, I don't give a shit. You're a real prick."

"Hey! Hey! Let's just forget it, okay?" Russ said, trying to cool tempers.

"No, fuck this guy," Ethan said, then turned his attention back to Lind. "We invite you to come play here with us, a friendly game, and all you do is run your mouth. It's you against the world, isn't it?"

"You done?" Lind said, not waiting for an answer. "No foul. Check it."

Ethan shook his head and walked toward his man. There was no use arguing, he couldn't win. Russ held onto the ball and walked over to him, hoping to alleviate the sudden tension.

"Enough, huh? This is supposed to be fun." Russ paused, waiting for a sign that Ethan had collected himself. "Hey, if I wanted to fight I'd go home to my wife. Let's have some fun here and play ball, what do you say?"

Ethan nodded at Russ, trying to appease his fellow teacher, but it wasn't sufficient. Russ took another step in and talked directly at Ethan's ear. "You okay, kiddo? Look, don't let him get to you. We all know he's an asshole, hell, he knows he's an asshole, but you can't crack, kiddo. You crack, he wins."

Russ slapped Ethan on the back and tossed the ball back to Lind, ready for defense. Before he even caught the ball, Lind was driving to the hole, trying to catch everyone off guard. Ethan left his man at the very moment Lind leaped and extended his hand out for the layup. The quick start, a cheap move, a sucker punch really, brought Ethan's rage to a boil. He undercut Lind, throwing a forearm into his gut, just below his ribs. The move took Lind's legs out from under him and he came down hard, nearly denting the wood as he crashed to the floor.

Within seconds Lind was up and cursing, sweating and shouting in Ethan's face. Adrenaline spewed into his bloodstream, it was pure fight or flight. Ethan stood ten feet tall, with tunnel vision, and tunnel hearing. Like a hunter staring through the scope of his rifle, Ethan zeroed in on Lind who was waving his hands and pointing his finger at him, tapping him repeatedly on the chest. Lind's finger, prodding Ethan's sternum, was enough to break the damn, the tipping point. Ethan swung, connecting with Lind's nose. Instantly, there was blood falling from Lind's nostril, but it didn't seem to faze him. Before he even reacted to the sight of his own blood, before he even dabbed his own face, Lind threw a hook into Ethan's ear, knocking him off balance. With his equilibrium unsteady, and knees laboring for balance, Ethan stumbled backwards.

Russ grabbed Ethan by the shoulders as the others jumped in to separate the two men. He pushed Ethan ten feet backward and slammed him against the wall. Sound and vision instantly returned, flooding Ethan's senses with the riotous scene.

"What are you thinking, kiddo!?" Russ was screaming and shaking Ethan. "You can't pull that shit here! You've got a job! You've got a responsibility, damn it!" Russ was confused and filled with a multitude of questions for his young friend. He cared for him, clearly, and he could tell, now more than ever, how lost he actually was. Clues were jumping out, practically glowing: Sunken, hallowed cheeks stained teeth and protruding bones.

"Get yourself together, kiddo." Russ struggled, searching for the right combination of words that would break through Ethan's head. He came up empty.

Ethan jerked himself free of Russ's grip, and spat on the floor in Lind's direction, trusting that he got the message. The gym was quiet as Ethan walked away, and the silence felt vast, heavy. But to Ethan it was loud, the silence. And its enormity was a burden, like the silence were an object that had been filled with a thousand screaming souls, each one louder than the last, and together their cries were a needle pressing deep inside his ear.

In the car, Ethan held the wheel so tight that the veins on the back of his hand began to throb. He sat facing the entrance to the school, half expecting Lind to come charging out of the double doors with a group of cop buddies, slapping Billy-clubs in their hands and looking for war. His hand started to tremble on the wheel so he took it off, stretched his fingers out, and started the car. As he opened and closed his fist, he could see the swelling develop. He prayed nothing was broken from the punch. He didn't want to give Lind Kirby that satisfaction.

145

The car stayed in park. Ethan didn't know where to go or what to do. He replayed the fight in his mind, beat by beat, reminding himself that his actions were warranted. Lind Kirby was an asshole. Lind Kirby was provoking him. Lind Kirby deserved it. And then there was Russ. Ethan wondered if Russ would stick up for him, wondered whose side he would take when the news reached Fenske, which it definitely would. He remembered Russ stepping in and taking Ethan by the shoulders, driving him into the wall, and how there was a look of abandonment in Russ's eyes. It stuck with Ethan, frightening him, as though he were too far gone, beyond help. Russ was brave and strong willed, never willing to quit on anyone or anything. Yet, with that look, most assuredly, he'd given up on Ethan. For the first time Ethan admitted to himself that his co-worker had actually been somewhat of a father figure, at least while at Park View Elementary. A father figure as a positive role model? It was an oxymoron in Ethan's life. That admission made the look Russ had in his eye all the more daunting. There was terror and devastation in that look. Not for himself, but for Ethan. It was all for Ethan. Russ feared for him because for the first time he saw there was nothing he could do, no words could be said. Ethan was outside the help of a friend. He had seen that look only once before, on his sister Rachel, just days before their father passed.

OCTOBER 18

A healthy gust of wind blew between the homes and smacked against him as he crossed the alley. The gust was cold and it stung his ear, the same ear that had stopped Lind's knuckles earlier that morning. It was still tender to the touch. The sky was still overcast, and the clouds were thicker than they'd been when he left the gym just a few hours earlier. They looked heavy, like they wanted to drop right down and settle among the fallen leaves for a lazy afternoon nap. Rather than leave his car at home and walk to his sisters, Ethan parked on the north side of Tower Grove, just a few doors down the street from Rachel's house.

Rachel was on the porch, emptying a watering can into her potted succulents, when she saw Ethan on the sidewalk and waved.

"What are you wearing shorts for? It's flippin' cold out, little brother," she said as he approached her front steps.

Ethan was still in his basketball clothes. He hadn't changed, he hadn't been home to change, in fact all he did do was drive around the city, from strip mall parking lot, to movie theater parking lot, to grocery store parking lot. He sat in each one, replaying the fight and the words he had said, wondering exactly what, and how bad the collateral damage was going to be when all the dust had settled. Jacob Kirby was his favorite student, and now he'd gone and broken the kid's fathers nose (he hoped it was broken, anyway). Lind was an asshole, but he wasn't a pussy. Ethan had a hard time imagining the prick would press charges, after all, he swung too. But he was a tough guy, a meat head, and he was a cop. Lind was more likely to bend the law before he would use the system against a special education school teacher. Ethan figured Lind might just show up at the duplex late one night, maybe he'd wait for Ethan to get out of the car, and then Lind would rough him up a bit - blacken an eye, crack a rib, that sort of thing - just to prove a point. He could get away with it too, the south side of the park having the reputation that it had. Crimes of that nature happened all the time, and frequently without any witnesses.

"Played ball this morning," Ethan said. "Didn't get a chance to shower yet. Thank you for meeting me." He jogged up the stairs, not wasting any time, and he was bouncing from toe to toe, full of anxious energy.

"Of course," she said, emptying the last of the water into a pot. "You were a bit cryptic on the phone, though. What's up?"

"Winslow home?"

"I told you he's in the studio till late tonight. What's going on with you?" For the first time, Rachel allowed herself to be alarmed, if only slightly.

Ethan walked past her and into the house, through the dining room, into the kitchen. He shuffled through the refrigerator until he found a cold bottle of beer, popped it open, and sat at the

148

table, staring out the back door into her yard, into the deep gray sky.

Rachel took off her wool jacket and slung it over the back of one of the other chairs at the kitchen table. Without the loose-fitting winter coat hiding her figure, she was showing. Ethan couldn't help but notice the subtle roundness of her pregnant belly and how it, just noticeably, pushed against her sweater. He was lost in the shape of her little hump, in the new way she moved about her kitchen space, in the reality that there was a child growing beneath that sweater. Quickly, he ran the numbers and assumed she must've still been in her first trimester, ten or eleven weeks. She carried herself with a confidence he hadn't seen before. Rachel had always been a strong and independent woman, but this was different, she had nothing to prove, she could just *be*. She now had the freedom to *be* herself, to exist as a beautiful woman, a happy wife, and an expectant mother.

"You're pregnant."

"No shit."

"I mean, I know, but... but now I can see. I can see it."

"I'm fucking fat already." Rachel was moving around the kitchen, cleaning, straitening things. She pulled a glass down from the cupboard and set it on the counter. "Gonna have to get new clothes soon, huh? Elastic waistbands for the next seven months. Real sexy."

"It looks good on you. Being pregnant. You look pretty."

"Fuck off."

"I'm serious," Ethan said. He was almost smiling. "You look pretty. And happy."

"Well..." She was momentarily caught off guard by such a complement coming from her brother, but she could see he was genuine, and the tenderness in his voice allowed her to accept it as truth. "Thank you."

149

Rachel removed the cork from an already opened bottle of red wine that had been tucked away on the corner of the counter, next to the jars of coffee and sugar. Ethan's eyes were still on her, watching her carry the bottle toward the empty glass she'd set out. He sat up straight, and with a sudden shift to anger and accusation in his voice, he questioned her.

"What are you doing?"

"Don't look at me like that," Rachel said, pouring the wine into the glass. "Like I'm some deadbeat mother. Doctor Holly says I can do one small glass a day and she knows her shit better than you or I. She's fine with it, I'm fine with it. The baby's fine with it."

"A day?" Ethan said, astounded by her proclamation.

"I don't have one every day, relax. Once a week. Two times, maybe."

She took a sip and they stared at each other in silence for a handful of seconds, the way close family members do from time to time. He took a drink of his beer and found his attention drifting back outside, through the window. Rachel joined Ethan at the table, sitting next to him, staring at his profile. It was clear his mind was in the throes of working through something significant. She could see tension in the wrinkles stretching out across his forehead, and the fatigue it was causing on his eyeballs. He was worn out, haggard looking.

"Hey…Hey," she said softly, trying to lasso his attention. There was no reply. Ethan took another drink and eyed the shifting clouds in the sky. "Hey… Brother." For the first time she was taking clear inventory of his physicality, and it was discomforting. "You don't look good. You feeling okay? Did you go out last night or something?"

Again, there was no reply. But his breathing began to change. Ethan took slow breaths inward, and pushed them out quickly through his nose, holding off as long as he could before pulling more oxygen into his lungs. It was as if he had to ditch the air quickly because hanging on too long could be deadly, and the moments of serenity, pure contentment and comfort, came only when he was neither inhaling nor exhaling. His eyes got wet and he blinked twice to fight off tears.

"She took my whole life with her," he said, finally breaking the silence.

"Hey, hey," she said, rubbing the tips of her fingers up and down his back. "Things are going to be okay."

"Yeah? I'm glad you're seeing the light, because from where I'm sitting things are looking pretty goddamn grim."

A blue jay landed on the deck's railing outside and it held Ethan's attention while he sifted through all that was circling his brain, deciding how much to divulge. The bird was holding something in its mouth, a bug of some sort, and it turned its head from side to side as it dismembered the insect into manageable bites.

"It's infectious," he said after the blue jay had finished his meal and flown away. "I got this classroom full of kids that are afraid to look at me, afraid to look me in the eye right now. Like if they look too close or look at me too long, this thing, this, this, this devil she left inside of me, is gonna suck them down too. The bell rings and they leave feeling like a bag of shit. Like me, sis. I can see it on them. Like there's this cloak of pain or shame that Mr. Atkinson is handing out every hour on the hour. Bell rings: 'Here ya go kids, the world is a piece of shit, enjoy.'" Ethan took a long drink and set the empty bottle down on the table off to the side, away from him. "And you know, it's fucked up, but I manage to take a little comfort in that. Like the little bit I give to them is a little bit that I don't have to deal with anymore. I know it's not true but it feels that way, in the moment."

He was blinking rapidly, treading the water that was filling his eyes.

"Wins said you were acting different," Rachel said, still rubbing his back. "I feel bad. I haven't been there for you. I haven't been a good sister."

"It's not about you," he said, turning toward her for the first time. "It's not about you! Don't take my shit and make it about you. It has nothing to do with how you feel, this is how I feel, what I'm going through."

When he stopped yelling the room was completely still. Ethan stood up, grabbed this empty beer bottle by the neck, and tossed it in the trash. Then he opened another. Rachel hadn't moved, her eyes were stuck on the wood grains in her kitchen table, the dark colors, the light colors, the various stains the table had acquired. Her brother's situation had taken her by surprise. She'd been ignorant to Ethan's condition, in the dark all this time (due both to his secrecy and her neglect), and now, suddenly she felt there was a bomb with a ticking clock on the other side of the kitchen that she needed to diffuse. Does she pull the red wire or the green? How big of an explosion could there be? Then she wondered how many smaller bombs had already been set off, and how much damage had already occurred.

"Winslow said you seemed upset the other night." She spoke slowly, choosing her words carefully. "And it made me realize that I haven't made myself totally available to you. But I'm here now. And it's clear you want to talk because you called me earlier, and you came here. You're here now. I'm here. And I'm listening."

Ethan sat back down at the table and stared outside. "Well, it's nice of you both to show so much concern." He took a drink and reached inside the pockets of his gym shorts. The tears were gone from his eyes, swallowed up by the anger. In the palm of his hand, he rolled two orange pill capsules back and forth. "I'm fine. Really. I'll be fine."

152

The show was for Rachel's benefit, moving the pills around like that in plain sight, begging for her to ask all about them. She took the bait.

"What is that?" she asked, knowing she'd given him exactly what he wanted.

"Pills," he said, popping them in his mouth and washing them down with the beer. "Anti-depressants," he said. Turning his head slowly, he stared at her, challenging her to respond, to warn him, to reach out and help him, to do or say something that showed she still loved and cared for him, that she would fight to save him even if he'd already thrown in the towel. Rachel said nothing. "What are you going to do, judge me now? You still have your son," he said, throwing daggers, trying to land them deep into her vital organs.

"Don't do that," she said softly, looking down again at the table. "Don't make me a victim in all this. I shouldn't have to feel bad for being a mother. I know you're in pain. And I am very sorry for that, Eth. I don't know what you're going through and I'm not going to pretend that I do. So if you want to take pills for a little while, if that's what helps you, then you should do that."

Rachel hadn't touched her wine except to push the glass further away. Inside the kitchen, it was silent again, but outside the wind was still blowing and wind chimes from the neighbor's yard were clanging and clashing together.

"It's dad and Janet's anniversary," Ethan said after a few more minutes of quiet.

"Why do you remember that? How do you remember that kind of shit?"

"I'm a teacher. Important dates are like thirty percent of the job." Ethan took a drink and leaned back, still looking outside.

"*Important*?" Rachel said with a muffled laugh. Finally, she lifted her eyes from the table. "You should call her," she said, flippant.

153

"I did. Voicemail."

"Well, I'm not going to. She never gave a shit about you or me. She wanted to fix dad and when that job ended…" She let the sentence fade into the air, shaking her head, either disapproving or dismissing her next thought.

They both sat motionless, stewing in various memories of their father. Rachel thought of the later years, when things were broken, when he was broken. Towards the end of his life he had a favorite chair, and later a favorite shirt. Eventually he wore the shirt and sat in the chair and watched his favorite channel, only moving to piss and shit. His *favorites* only became favorites out of a lack of energy, or enthusiasm for anything requiring the smallest amount of effort. For instance, John Atkinson's favorite shirt became a favorite because it was easier continuing to wear that one rather than changing into a clean one. Bathing stopped and eating became a battle, something they forced onto him. And before the degradation of his general character, there was the violence, the spoons, and the belts. Fathers and mothers have an uncanny ability to infect their children with emotional sores. When their love disappears, their children are lost, left to find their own way. Things got bad quickly after Ethan was born. John had trouble looking either of his kids in the eye. And hugs, rare as they were in the Atkinson household, were open palmed pats on the back, not warm embraces with arms squeezing out affection.

At one point he was loving, tender, open hearted, and caring, a splendid father and a wonderful man. Then he lost his soul mate, and that man withered. His leaves became dry and brittle, sharp even. John was irritable and dangerous. Rachel felt she couldn't walk from one room to the next without an intense fear of upsetting her father. Spoons. Spoons. Spoons. Spoons. Spoons. The spoons where what left the deepest sores, the sores that puss and scab, and never fully heal. Even as an adult she couldn't eat cereal without thinking of the flick of his wrist and the sound that the slap of the cold metal made against her young skin.

After he remarried, when Janet came into the picture, his behavior remained unaltered, at least regarding Ethan and Rachel. She was nothing like their mother, Rachel remembered, nothing like her at all. Their mother would never condone John's lack of love and respect, both for himself, and his children. Janet enabled him, sympathized with his loss. She allowed him to be a victim, and she and John carried on as if Rachel and her toddler brother were nothing more than fish in a bowl, pets to be fed and then ignored, left to swim and fend for themselves.

Ethan on the other hand, was thinking differently. He thought in pictures, old pictures, before the anger and resentment had chiseled away at John's face. He saw smiling moments, when a young man stood with his new bride, holding hands as they posed for a photo on the porch of their first house; or his dad sporting a mustache, one hand on the roof of an old green mustang, the other holding a soapy sponge, while fresh water flowed from the hose at his feet. Photos were all he could use to build an image of his father. There were small scenes, a feeling, a glimpse of a time when he could remember his dad as a breathing human, but mostly, it was through photos. With photos he drew the conclusions he wanted, painting John into the kind of dad Ethan needed him to be. Ethan was six when his father died. Everything before that was a blur. The pictures helped put things in focus, albeit inaccurate.

"Looks like the temperature is dropping," Ethan said. The wind chimes were shaking wildly, making more noise than before.

Rachel didn't respond. She pressed her glass up to her lips and drank less than a Holy Communion's shot worth of wine. She didn't want it anymore, but it was there.

"Does Winslow have a jacket I can borrow," Ethan said standing up from the table and walking back to the refrigerator. "A sweatshirt or something?"

"Yeah, I'm sure. There's usually one on the hook, by the door." She looked over at him, watched him take another bottle out of the refrigerator, but leave it unopened. "Are you going for a run?"

"No."

"Then what?"

"I don't know. A drive. I've been driving a lot lately. It's peaceful."

"Where do you wanna go?"

Ethan released a deep sigh. Winslow's jacket was on and zipped up, the neck of the beer sticking out of his pocket. "I'm fine," he said.

"I know you're fine. But I wanna go with you. You can drive my car," Rachel said, preparing herself to leave. "I've got heated seats."

They kept the music off, preferring to drive in silence, listening to the hum of the tires beneath them, and the whispers of passing cars. Ethan was only going fifty, westbound down interstate forty-four. When they passed Hampton Boulevard, Ethan pulled the bottle from the jacket pocket, opened it, checked his side mirrors for Fuzz, and took a drink. He kept the bottle tucked between his legs while driving, concealing his misdemeanor. Rachel watched, knowing she should stop him, but too scared of another outburst to question his actions. She wondered how far he planned on going down the highway; forty-four cut westward across the entire state of Missouri. They were already out of South City and Ethan had given no indication where they were headed, or if he even knew. Rachel figured they'd cruise the Tower Grove neighborhoods or maybe take a drive through Forest Park, which was always so beautiful in October, leaves shedding and changing colors in the brisk autumn air, but they had passed that exit and were approaching Webster Groves, she could see the University ahead on her right.

"Have you thought about anyone new yet? Dating?" Rachel said, failing at an attempt to be casual with her words. She just wanted to get him talking. His silence and slow-lane driving were beginning to creep her out.

"No." He was lying.

"Yeah. Too soon, I guess. I just thought, I dunno…" She looked out her window, staring at the pictures on the billboards. "A fling or something. I dunno..."

"No. I wouldn't know what to do."

The car slowed down to forty five, forty, then he hit the blinker, and faded onto the exit ramp, toward Elm Street. Rachel sat up in the passenger seat, put one hand on her belly, while gripping the door with the other.

"Are you scared?" He took a drink and looked squarely at her after he asked the question.

"Hmm?" Rachel pretended not to hear the question. The truth was, she didn't understand why he would ask that. She was scared, yes, but she didn't want to admit it and certainly couldn't pin point exactly why. 'Hmm' is what came out, hoping he'd clarify himself.

"To have him. To have a baby. Does it scare you?"

Ethan put the left blinker on as the car came upon the intersection at Elm Street, and Rachel knew instantly where her brother was going. Her fear shifted. Now she felt scared for Ethan. She pitied him, and she was suddenly glad that she'd offered to come along for the ride. She could be there for him, protect him.

"I'm fucking terrified. You know I am." Rachel said, taking her hand off her belly, and placing it on her brother's shoulder. "But I gotta believe we're all gonna be okay. And I gotta believe I'm gonna know what I'm doing, even though I don't. At all."

Ethan made the left turn and the road became bumpy. The wheels bounced over poorly covered pot holes and tar seams. "Where we going, Eth?" Rachel asked, already knowing the answer.

He smiled back at her and took a drink from the bottle of beer. "Paying our respects, Rach."

Within minutes the car was parked and they were walking among the tall oak trees and overgrown grass of St. Paul Cemetery. The sun had fallen off the horizon causing the temperature to dip again. Ethan was glad he'd borrowed the jacket, though he wished he'd gotten pants as well. The skin on his legs was dry and cold. They navigated the freshly laid flowers and headstones until they reached the one that belonged to their mother. Standing over her plot, they shivered with a mixture of emotions. The chilly, gray weather sent goose pimples up Ethan's bare legs.

Katherine Elizabeth Atkinson
April 3rd 1945
December 12th 1976

She was young, just two years older than Ethan was now. Rachel had already outlived her. There were no flowers at the base of the grave and it bothered Rachel. She began walking around nearby plots and thieving a single flower from each arrangement. "Give me a hand, will ya," she said, bending at her knees so as not to crunch the baby.

"You're stealing flowers from dead people?"

"They don't need them." Rachel had already accumulated a variety for her bouquet.

"And mom does?"

"Just help me, damnit."

"Why?" Ethan said, finally turning to address his sister. "Tell me why I should steal flowers for *her* instead of doing it for...

Rosemary Hayes?" he said, reading and gesturing to the stone next to their mothers. "Why not Rosemary Hayes? I know about as much about Rosemary Hayes as I do Katherine Atkinson. We've spent exactly the same amount of time together. Why not Norma Garner, or Robert and Margaret Walsh?" He was walking around from headstone to headstone, gesticulating and shouting to prove his point.

Rachel's hand fell to her waist side, as if giving up on the idea of a bouquet. "She is your mother," she said as she started walking back toward Ethan.

"No, Rach, she's your mother!"

"She gave birth to you!" Rachel was exasperated. She was pleading with him, her fear driving every word. But he was still storming around, moving his limbs wildly, shouting his responses across the cemetery.

"Yeah, she gave birth to me. Then what? Then what!?" Ethan marched back toward their mother's grave. "Do you see that? Do you see that, Rach?" he demanded an answer. "December 12th, 1976. That's my fucking birthday, right there. That's my birthday printed on that stone."

"I know, Ethan," Rachel said. Her knees were trembling. "I was there too."

"That is a rock. That's all it is to me," he continued. "A rock with some letters on it, that's all. She was *your* mother, not mine. She was never there. She was never there..." His voice was shaky from the nerves in his throat, and every so often he would tremble, shiver like a naked body stuck out in the snow.

In an uncalculated moment, acting from the hatred in his gut, the hatred fueled by multiple abandonments, Ethan pulled the string on his shorts and released the knot. Reaching his hand inside, he gripped his penis and lifted it over the waistband, spreading his legs slightly, preparing to urinate. Rachel dropped the bouquet and ran toward him, shouting, commanding him to stop. She threw all her weight into him, slapping him and knocking him off balance. "What the fuck are you thinking, Eth?!" She collided with him again, arms outstretched, knocking him to the ground. Tears pushed past her rage and poured down her face. "Where are you, brother?" she said, standing above him, wiping her eyes and holding her round stomach. "Where are you?"

"She was never there for me..." he mumbled. Ethan's face was red, his eyes puffy and swelling with tears.

Rachel knelt in the grass and gathered her brother in her arms. She was hopeless and distraught, lost in how to proceed. She was in the dark when it came to Ethan's situation. Rachel had spent the majority of her life keeping watchful eye over her brother, always looking over her shoulder to make sure he was ok, and that he would survive, parentless, to be a strong and independent man. And here he was, broken at the foot of his mother's grave. She tried not to blame herself. How could she have known how far he'd fallen? In her heart, she knew his wounds were deep, too deep to fix on his own, but watching him suffer was a torment that would cripple her bones. She had no idea how to be there for him, she knew only to hold him, like a child, and rock him until his tears were dry.

OCTOBER 18

They kissed and hugged in the alley outside of her garage. Rachel had driven home so Ethan could rest. Even though it was a short trip, ten miles more or less, he nearly fell asleep several times, resting his head on the cold glass window, nodding off and waking up whenever the car hit a bump in the road. His eyes would open and he'd see himself though the passenger side mirror. The circles beneath his eyes were deep and dark, like they'd been hallowed out with lumps of charcoal. He'd look away, at passing cars, or building landmarks, or the red white and green Italian flags hanging from light poles as they passed through 'The Hill', but his gaze would always land back on the frightening image in the mirror, his ghost. Ethan was anxious to get back to his own car. He wanted to be home, to sleep at least twelve hours, and when he woke, he would start to get his life back in order.

As he was holding his sister in his arms, Ethan tried to put a positive spin on the afternoon. Maybe he had hit the bottom and maybe the bottom needed to be hit. Maybe now he could call Maggie, in the morning after the long sleep, see if she'd like coffee, see if they could treat each other like people again and forget about the weeks after the abortion, when they were zombies walking around their old duplex, ready to suck the life out one another, ready to lash out at the slightest disturbance. Maybe he could pull himself together and get her to see what made them both so happy for so many years.

When Rachel let go and turned to her house, Ethan saw that her face was different than earlier in the afternoon. She'd taken on his sadness. He was contagious, and just like with the children at school, he took solace in being able to alter her mood.

Misery craving company.

He didn't like what he'd done, he didn't like that he'd raped her of the strength she showed while walking around her kitchen just several hours before, but it was god damned comforting to have someone empathize, to have someone understand with their own feelings, with their own misery, what he was experiencing.

He felt a notch better. He even raised his head up to the sky as he walked back to his own car. The clouds overhead were ominous, swelling with an impatience to collapse down on the earth below. There was no break in them, just a billowy thickness, waiting to drop rain for hours, days even, and release all that had built within. The vomitus orange streetlights kicked on just as he turned the key to start the engine.

Inside his duplex, Ethan flopped onto the couch and set the cigar box and plate out on the coffee table. The rain had finally started to fall and he heard its patter against the roof as he stared at the logo on the box's lid. He sat for several minutes waiting, longing for the thrill that used to accompany this very ritual. It was

162

gone. What was once a cherished moment, a joyous to escape, had spiraled into an insatiable desire, a reflex, a vital need no different than pulling in oxygen and releasing carbon dioxide. The ritual lost its purpose when the high became the answer.

Suddenly the problem was as clear as a country day. He tossed the weed and the cigar box back into the drawer.

Ethan made a phone call. It lasted only seconds, but he paced the living room throughout the conversation, like he was waiting on test results from a doctor. He wrote an address on the back of an opened envelope and when he finished, he threw on some clothes, a raincoat, and locked the door behind him.

•

Her apartment was a half mile in the wrong direction, into the forbidden Benton Park. But with the rain pouring and his hood drooped over his head, he figured he looked as scary as anyone he might encounter. Still, he walked the whole way with two keys protruding between his fingers, the household brass knuckle/switchblade hybrid.

Tammy was indifferent when she answered the door, she didn't say hello or wave, she merely acknowledged him with a half-smile, and turned back into her cave, leaving Ethan to let himself in and lock up.

He stepped in a few feet and straightened a frame that was mounted crooked on the wall by the front door. The laughing couple in the photo caught him off guard. Tammy wasn't the young girl smiling at the camera. This face belonged to a model, the everyday-girl-next-door model. And the man next to her, laughing, had perfect teeth, perfect hair, his sweater had no pills. They were on a picnic and someone had captured this perfect loving moment. It was all staged. In the bottom corner of the picture Ethan finally saw the barcode that had been looming.

Tammy had hung the picture of the happy couple used to sell that very frame. He looked quickly around the living room. There were more, at least two that he could see. She'd surrounded herself with pictures of other people's happy moments. Fake happy moments, at that.

A series of distinct and unpleasant smells pulled him away from the phony photos. His nose drew his eyes to the litter box, which sat on the floor next to the TV. Her television chest was a dinosaur, measuring at least 60 inches from the floor. It was the first of its kind, the pioneer of home entertainment, a luxury in the early 90's, now rejected without hesitation by Good Will or Salvation Army. The thing, this so called TV, assaulted her living room with all its glory. It was all so odd, he thought, the living room litter box, the television, the photos, but then again, little he knew about Tammy *was* ordinary, and he accepted that fact.

He looked around the place where Tammy lived. It was devastating. *How did I get here?* And why did he accept it like a conviction? There were magazines with address labels unassigned to her or the address on her apartment, stolen from neighbors or doctors' offices. Full ashtrays. Half empty, dented cans of diet coke. Clutter. On the arm of the couch, a black, tailless cat scraped its rough tongue against dirty panties. There was left over food crusting itself to a paper plate. A candle, dripping wax into abstract art, burnt the last of its wick on the top of the massive television box. Ethan accepted it all without judgment.

Maggie started creeping into his brain again, her sweet floral smell, her perfect teeth, the tiny blonde hairs on the small of her back. He longed to be in his own place, for her to be there playing records and dancing in her pencil skirt. He wanted that normalcy.

Tammy had a cigar box of her own and it was sitting open in the center of the coffee table. Ethan had never seen heroin before but he knew what it was in an instant. The brown powder, the spoon, the lighter, the sterile plastic-wrapped syringe, all the tools needed to evaporate for hours. His heart started pounding against his sternum. The box called to him, pulling him in. Somehow, knowing all of heroin's dangers made it all the more intriguing. He'd never tried it before. He was curious.

Tammy came back to the living room holding a plate of quartered, grilled cheese sandwiches, and the sandwiches were in a circle surrounding a mound of mayonnaise.

"Sorry. I had to use the butts," she said. "There wasn't enough bread." She elbowed the cat off the couch but left the panties alone.

Tammy was wearing an old sweatshirt with the collar ring cut off, and matching sweatpants. She looked as sexy as anyone possibly could in a pair of old sweats. The cotton dripped off her curves, hiding her body but hinting at all the goodness and pleasure it had to offer. There was an aggressive looking bird mascot ironed onto the upper thigh, it matched the one across the chest. Even though Tammy wasn't exactly athletic, he figured the sweat suit was hers from high school. She didn't have the mentality for competitive sports. Her interests were in other things: the arts, politics, books, theater. But her body, the shape of her calves, the strength of her thighs when they wrapped around his waist…she could've played soccer. Ethan stood on the opposite side of the room, and thought about her, about where she came from and how she grew up, how she ended up in this landfill apartment in the Benton Park ghetto. He thought about her in those sweats, kicking a soccer ball around tiny orange practice cones. For a moment he wanted to be seventeen again, French kissing afterschool in some abandoned hallway filled with lockers.

She set the food on the table and moved her heroin box off to the side with the back of her hand, very nonchalant. Tammy knew he'd seen what was inside but she didn't care, she wasn't trying to hide anything. That's what made her so devastatingly

165

attractive – she didn't withhold her dark secrets, she didn't save them for a 'special someone' or make a man work to break down her walls. Tammy would rather punch you in the mouth with it, repeatedly, just to see how much you could take.

"Are you hungry?" she said, offering up a square.

Ethan walked over to her, took it from her hand, and dipped it into the mayonnaise. He tried to eat it casually, with confidence, but there was too much trepidation shaking his bones. Short bursts of pain shot from his knuckles to his wrist as he ate the sandwich. It was impossible to ignore the swelling and discoloration that had settled in after the punch. He wondered what Lind told Jacob, if he was still Jacob's favorite teacher. If he was ever Jacob's favorite teacher.

"Take your coat off," she said. "Stay a while."

Tammy took it off for him and threw it on a pile of clothes that she'd been building in the corner of her living room. She grabbed his good hand and pulled him onto the couch. He sensed she was working toward something, trying to gather all of his attention for some big speech. Touching his face with her hands, she pulled gently and turned his head so they were eye to eye. Her face was kaleidoscopic, changing colors with the flickering images of the TV screen.

"I think I love you," she said without an ounce of love in her voice. It was a test, not an expression of emotion. Her eyes were like fishhooks, floating in the water, waiting to set the trap.

"I love you too." He didn't mean it but he said it anyway, and he said it quickly. It was a defensive reaction. Six thousand five hundred fifty two times Maggie had said *I love you,* and somewhere near the nine hundredth time, *I love you too,* became a general reactionary response to the meaningful/meaningless phrase.

Tammy knew he was lying too, but she didn't care. He gave the right answer. She would be safe with him, at least for the night. "Good. I was worried that that might scare you away." She took another square, dipped it, and fed him.

He was scared, like a dog with its tail tucked deep between its hind legs, but not of her, of himself. He was scared of his rapidly transforming morals, and character. The past summer seemed like a lifetime ago, when he was eating dinner and singing songs in round with his family: Rach and Wins cracking jokes, Maggie's sensitive, delicate fingertips. Four lousy months later, he's sitting on a couch with a sheet covering god knows what, in an ashtray of an apartment - *the fucking walls have cancer* - with a box of cat shit in front of him, and a box heroine by his side. This new life was a cruel mistress with a loose cunt and a tight whip.

"Why do you love me?" he asked.

"Why does anybody love anybody?" she countered.

Tammy had answered his question with another question: Socratic questioning. She'd taken his teaching methods and used them against him. For years, since first studying Socrates in college, he embraced the method to further probe his students and friends. Turning the question around forced a deeper level of thought, and it was a brilliant trick to guide his students to find an answer on their own. But from her, it didn't feel right. She was lying, she didn't love him, she just needed to validate her decisions, validate the time they'd spent together.

"I guess, because…" he spoke softly, taking her hands in his. "Because we all, deep down, just want to be touched. And through love, you get that."

"I like when you touch me," Tammy said, with a tiny smile curling up from the corner of her lips. Ethan slid the sleeve of her sweatshirt up past her elbow. He turned her wrist upward and ran the edge of his nails against her pale, white skin. His eyes followed his hands, looking closely at veins and freckles.

167

"You won't find anything." She was direct, bordering on harsh. Ethan raised an eyebrow, pretending not to know what she was talking about. "Tracks," she said.

Suddenly, a voice from the television bombarded his ears. The man was abrasive, forward, and he was selling cars. Ethan turned toward the TV, still holding her wrist in his hands. Tammy reached for the remote, pressed power, and the man selling cars behind a podium shrunk into a white dot. The room was quiet. Tammy leaned back on the couch arm, resting her head where the cat had been licking her dirty black underwear.

She stared at Ethan for a long beat and then finally asked if it frightened him, the box. He said it didn't.

"I hoped it would bother you." She started rubbing the bottom of her bare feet on his legs. "If you're not cool with it, I can wait. Till later, or something."

"Do you use it a lot?" he asked.

She shook her head. "Just special occasions."

"And what, pray tell, is the occasion?"

"Pray tell? Jesus."

"I was raised by my grandmother." Ethan crossed his arms and legs and sat back into the couch. "Sorry." When he moved, her foot fell away from him.

"Don't be," she said.

It was quiet again, the candle on the TV danced, throwing shadows across the wall.

"My Grandma used to say 'Jeepers' all the time," Tammy said. Her foot found his leg again, rubbing the tip of her toe on the inseam of his jeans, down near the ankle.

"Our first time together," she said, smirking again. "That's the occasion."

Ethan didn't balk. She had such confidence in him and its effect was calming. He could feel his heart settle into his chest, the pounding had subsided. It was pumping slowly, with ease, and

168

each beat covered him more fully in Tammy's sticky web, the web that collected all her prey, one at a time. Numerous men had struggled to free themselves in the past, and eventually they'd all given up, forced to succumb to her overwhelming power. They'd dry out while she devoured their insides, sucking their life away like the custard filling of a devilish dessert. Ethan was next, he told himself, looking deep into her eyes. For the first time he noticed them, grey, colorless. He was stuck and struggling, but he wasn't sure how much longer he could continue to fight.

"You should eat a little more." Tammy took another square and handed it to him. "It won't be as bad if you throw up."

She stood up and walked to her bedroom after he swallowed the first bite. Ethan looked around the room again, taking inventory of the smaller details, trying to imagine himself living in such a state of disarray. He thought about her parents, and the sadness they'd surely feel if they dropped in on their daughters living quarters. If she even had parents. But there was freedom in her lifestyle, in the carelessness projected across her apartment. She gave the finger to society, to convention and conformity. Tammy was a radical, whether forced into her shit existence by nature or nurture, she wore the leather jacket and black denim of rebellion, and she wore it well. The cat was asleep and dreaming. Ethan watched its frail whiskers twitch about.

Deep, slow, carnal music came out from bedroom and marched on a steady beat to fill the living room. Tammy walked back through the doorway wearing only her bra and panties. Nothing erotic: a sports bra, black, and some colorful cotton covering her bottom parts. She stood tall before him, her navel at his face, and began running her hands through his greasy, messy hair, digging her nails into his scalp. He melted, tossing his head back, acting just like her cat. He did everything but purr. When she stopped, his head came forward, and he started licking the spot on her underwear where he assumed her clit might be. She moaned for a half second, and then stopped him.

"It feels good, but…no."

Ethan looked up, confused. The candle, the music, she was half naked for Christ's sake.

"I wanna show you," she said. "I've never shown anyone."

"Okay."

Tammy turned her knee out and opened her inner thigh, exposing a patch of bruised skin. There was a red dot in the center of the discoloration. "It's the highway," she said in a whisper. "Gets it to your heart faster. Nothing is wasted." She was silent, waiting for his response, but he had none. "Does it gross you out? I've never shown anyone, say something, damn it."

Without hesitation, he kissed the mark with wet lips and an open mouth, his hands on her ass to pull her in tight and control her. Ethan was impulsive, bordering on reckless, but he couldn't resist. It was more than sex, more than a desire to be inside her body, he wanted inside her mind. She was already inside his.

"I'm going to take care of you. I promise," she said. She could be so convincing when she wanted to.

As Ethan took his shirt off and lay across the couch, he wondered if he would hate her again, like last time. He wondered if, when he came, he'd want her to disappear, to vanish, to leave her own apartment, to be anywhere but near him, die if need be. Last time, the moment he finished her face changed. All of her negative qualities came to the forefront: the enormous pores on her nose, the stubby eyebrow hairs that needed plucking, her fucking breath. He thought about this forthcoming hatred as she stood over him alongside the couch, looking like a school girl, innocent, pure, curious, wearing nothing more than a pair of cheap cotton underwear she'd probably purchased at Target.

But deep down, he knew she was none of those things. Tammy had seen it all. Her tongue was dull from tasting everything that life had to offer. She was over the whole thing, and this, this thing here with Ethan, was nothing but a game. Despite knowing all of this, he prepared himself for her.

"I'm going to take good care of you," she said again. "You don't have to be afraid."

Tammy sat on the coffee table with the cigar box resting on her knees. She tied off his arm and let the pressure built in his vein while she lit the spoon. She pulled the liquid into the syringe and Ethan closed his eyes. He could feel the adrenaline again, pushing his heart up into his throat.

"Okay," she said with a smile, taking his outstretched arm into her hands, "Relax. Momma's going to take everything away."

The needle pierced his flesh and she emptied it into him. In a flash, a wave of ice crashed down on his arm, paralyzing his upper body, and a blanket of fire covered his toes, his ankles, his calves. The opposing forces met somewhere around his waist, and they collided but they would not unite. Like oil and vinegar, the ice and fire in his veins remained distinct, powerful, full of strength and vigor. His eyes rolled back and then to the side. He gave in to the drugs console, wrapped himself in its womb, and set off to float carelessly, effortlessly down the river to a land without worry, without strife or tension, where disappointment was nonexistent, and contentment came easy.

Tammy kissed him and brushed the hair away from his eyes. She laid a blanket across his bare chest and tucked him to sleep, like any good mother would. Indeed, she took care of him, just as she'd promised.

OCTOBER 20

It was Monday morning, and the bedside radio alarm went off at 6:00 am on the button. Ethan didn't consciously register it as his *alarm* until 8:48 am. NPR's Morning Edition had been on for two hours forty eight minutes, and the voices carrying across air waves were taking on a life all their own inside his head, creating images and storylines with supposed hidden meanings as his dreams played out.

He was naked, in his own bed, and he pulled a pillow over his face when his eyes finally cracked open. There was so much sunlight screaming in through the bedroom window it was a wonder anyone could sleep as soundly as he had been sleeping. It was the traffic report that finally jarred him awake at 8:48 am. Forty eight minutes after the first period bell had rung at Park View Elementary. Ethan's earliest class wasn't technically until 10:00 am, but the entire faculty was required to arrive well before first period in order to prepare for the day, but also, and perhaps more importantly, so they could be available to the students should they have any questions or personal issues they'd like to speak with their teachers about.

Knowing, hoping rather, that he wasn't likely needed for another hour, he moved through his duplex with an apparent lack of urgency. Truth be told, he was recovering from one hell of a weekend, and the previous fourteen hours of sleep was easily the longest period of time he'd gone without a chemical in his body over the past fifty seven days. He wouldn't have moved with urgency if there had been a loaded gun pressed against his temples.

Park View Elementary's parking lot was full of cars and minivans, more crowded than a typical Monday. Someone was in his usual spot so he was forced to park further way, at the far end of the lot. He took his time getting to the building, walking between cars, peering into windows, and reading vanity plates. Some of the minivans had child-safety seats, others, he could see, were well lived in, with travel mugs, newspapers, and brief cases strewn about. They were family cars, most of them.

Once he was inside, he decided to avoid the administrative offices, wanting not to explain his tardiness, and instead head straight to his classroom. When he turned the corner, he saw students and parents sitting in chairs, lining the walls of the hallway.

He knew in an instant that he was fucked.

His sluggish pace quickened as Ethan began to panic. He pulled his cellular phone from his pocked to confirm the date and time: Monday, October 20th, 9:57 am.

No, it can't be, he said to himself, shaking his head, trying to clear the cobwebs. *It can't be, it can't be. The semester just started. I wouldn't have forgotten, I wouldn't let that happen.* He wanted to ignore the facts but the evidence was overwhelming. The parents were there for Mid Term Conferences. For Ethan, that meant IEU Reports. The Individualized Education Unit progress reports were to be presented with the students, parents, shrinks, and administrators all present, the whole god damn *Team*. And Ethan, the primary figure in the schools special education department, was late.

The panic was at full throttle. He raced to think of appropriate lies to cover his massive fuck up. *Traffic? Not at 10am. Accident? Maybe, but the first thing Fenske is gonna want to see is an incident report or, fuck, at least a trashed bumper. I could trash my bumper. If I beat it, knocked it off even, I might bruise, or bleed too. That would play into the story. No one questions blood. I could leave, get into an accident. Go to the hospital. Fenske wouldn't even visit. Whore. Pompous fucking whore! She's so god damn controlling. I can't leave. Too many witnesses already. But I didn't say hello, didn't even wave, maybe they wouldn't recognize me.*

Ethan approached his classroom door without an alibi. He'd have to tell the truth: *I slept in. Why? Well, Fenske, you overbearing cunt, I spent much of the weekend experimenting with a Morphine derivative, and the side effects lead to hours of self-medication. Then, satisfied with the results, I decided to let my body rest. What kind of drugs? Listen, that's unimportant. What is important are the facts, and the facts are that I am here, and I am clear headed, ready to help these students. Well, Mam, I am aware of how late I am, and yes I did set an alarm. As I already stated, I was resting. Unfortunately, I underestimated how much rest I truly needed, and yes, I am quite sorry for the slight negative impact this one, tiny, isolated event is going to have on the children. How are the children, by the way? I missed them this morning. Missed them dearly.*

It would have to work.

Before he could reach out and put his hand on the doorknob, it was already turning. The door swung open, narrowly

174

missing Ethan's face. Lind Kirby was exiting the room with his wife. Jake trailed close behind. They nearly collided in the doorway. There was a momentary standoff between them, both men wanting to finish what they'd started on Saturday, but both equally wanting to block the event from their memory. Lind was four inches taller and towering over Ethan as they passed each other in the hall. But the bandage covering his nose reminded him of Ethan's capabilities.

Everyone made nice – fake smiles and hellos – and Ethan apologized for missing their meeting. They left. The heavy door slammed behind them. The sound was thunderous in the empty classroom.

Ethan turned, another standoff. Fenske was behind his desk, sitting in his creaky old chair, and she wore a scowl, tired and full of disappointment, across her face. There were two chairs beside Ethan's desk, still warm from Lind and his wife. He grabbed the back of one of the chairs.

"Don't sit," Fenske commanded.

Ethan looked up, slightly taken aback with her intensity.

"This won't take long," she said, "So just stand there and listen to me. Can you manage that? These kids are number one priority, Mr. Atkinson. Number one. You know that. And nothing can jeopardize that. I understand you've had a rather difficult run the past couple months and I have been willing to let you process things in your own way."

She sat forward and spread her elbows wide on his desk, preparing to deliver the heart of her message. There would be no ambiguity. Fenske was firm and direct when the moment called for such. Ethan leaned his weight on the back of the chair, arms extended, propping him up. His legs were too weak to stand tall against her words.

"Mr. Atkinson, you're screwing things up. In big, big ways. It's no longer about you. You have made the choice to involve the students in your problems. These kids, the Special Education kids, they have all been dealt a crappy hand, and what they need more than anything else in the whole world is reliability. Someone they can count on, look up to, someone they can trust. You have to know in your heart that you're letting them down. Your personal life and the decisions you're making outside these walls are becoming a serious threat to these children. And I won't allow it to continue."

Fenske studied him, making sure he registered her tone and the severity of the forthcoming consequences. She had an abundance of sympathy for Ethan, and the compassion, or maybe it was pity, was evident. She'd heard rumors of his separation but knew little else surrounding his personal life. But ultimately, she knew his work, she knew the passion he had for teaching, and how genuinely he loved and cared for the children. And what made things so difficult for her now was that she could no longer see any of that behind his eyes. The life, the energy, was gone. The man she'd hired four years prior was completely unrecognizable. He had backed her into a corner and left her with only one option.

"Ethan, I need you to pack your things. You're terminated."

With that final word, terminated, the exclamation point to her monologue, he let go of the chair, and fell back a step until one of the student's desks caught him. He knew there was nothing that could be said or done to undo her decision. Once again, he blamed Maggie. Her selfish choice had led to this moment. If she only knew the repercussions for her actions, the penance that had been dumped upon him, the lives she had affected, ruined, ended. To Ethan, she was the culprit, the one responsible for everything. She was the devil and she tainted Ethan's world with her wickedness.

Fenske was relentless, ready to kick the man while he was down and licking his wounds. She opened her leather binder and removed a business card from the inside flap. "I think you should take this," she said. "You should seriously consider talking to someone before things get worse." With three fingers, she slid the card across his desk. The title, Psychologist, seemed to jump off the business card. "Doctor Sarah Tucker. She helped me work through my divorce. Just...consider it."

She looked at him for a minute, waiting for him to move or respond, defend himself, she would have accepted anything. But he gave her nothing, he merely rested against the tiny student desk behind him and kept his eyes wide and fixated on the business card, not looking at it really, in fact, not looking at anything, just dazed. Fenske closed her binder and walked toward the door, turning back to say goodbye or perhaps give a final reminder to pack up his desk and clear out, but she restrained herself, thought better of it, and simply sighed before turning again to leave him alone in the empty classroom. The bell rang outside in the hallway. It was 10:00 am.

•

It was marvelously depressing, Ethan recalled, how, whenever someone on television would lose their job, their entire career would always fit so seamlessly, so perfectly, into a cardboard box. It was never messy, and *never* did they need a second box. There were never friends to escort the TV star to their car, and complain about how unjust their boss had been. It was always simple. How could that be, he thought. How could years' worth of work be whittled down to, and summed up in, a brown cardboard box?

But on this day, the depression came from how eerily true to life those TV depictions had been. Only, there was plenty of room to spare inside his box. It was light, and he could have carried its contents with nothing more than two bare hands if he chose to. But there was strong imagery in the cardboard box -

carried under one arm by the helpless, newly unemployed, as they made their way through their former place of employment, pathetic little eyeballs at every turn, looking curiously from the corners of their ugly heads - so he filled the box with the few things he had: Far Sides calendar, Rubik's Cube, some pens and pencils, his graham cracker stash. And even though the stapler didn't technically belong to him, Ethan threw it in for good measure.

He refrained from looking over his shoulder as he walked out the door. Ethan refused to define his time at Park View, the time spent caring and nurturing students, by the moment he'd just shared with Principal Fenske. There was passion and technique and patience and love, enormous amounts of love, throughout his teaching career. And that is what he wanted to see when he closed his eyes and thought about his old classroom, his old creaky chair, the long row of windows opening to the grassy field and the world outside.

The bell rang again and its sound meant the time was 10:50 am. It went off at ten till and again on the hour. Parent/Teacher meetings were probably over, half-day for both students and faculty. The halls were empty and quiet. Everyone had left. The kids had all gone with their parents to spend their half-holiday with reruns and soap operas. Some were probably dropped off with grandma and grandpa, while the lucky few, the popular few, hung out in best friend's basements and played video games while their best friend's mother spread peanut butter and jelly across slices of white Wonder bread.

Yet, as clear as the bell rang in Ethan's ear, so were the sounds of the students laughing and talking, pushing and passing notes, their tiny footsteps rushing down the hall toward their next class. As he walked down the empty hallway, cardboard box in hand, he maneuvered around the mirage of students huddling beside their lockers. He pulled the box in close to his ribs so as not to catch a corner on one of their small, young heads.

178

Would another school take him, he wondered. *Surly Fenske wouldn't withhold a referral,* though she didn't offer one. *She's stern but not vindictive. One stupid fucking meeting! I missed one meeting, and you're gonna fire me*? As he walked past her office he began a whole litany of responses, things he wished he would have said, ways he could have fought back, recalling moments throughout his tenure that stood out and could prove how deserving he was of a second chance. But in the end, he was angry with himself and angry at Fenske for not standing by his side, and he knew another meeting, at least at this time, would only lead to further destruction. *It was a parent meeting. One lousy parent meeting. They send their kids to me because they don't know how to handle them, they don't know how to teach them. These kids have problems that I am specialized in dealing with. I've got a track record of happy, healthy fucking students. What the fuck does she know, Fenske, sitting behind a fancy desk in a goddamn office, away from the kids, from everybody. She's an administrator! She only wishes she had my ability, my talent. Good luck finding another replacement.* But he knew. He knew he was wrong and knew he had only himself to blame, himself and Maggie. Yet, he was angry, and his anger bred a violent and abusive internal exchange.

The student's voices faded away when he noticed there were still a few faculty members lingering around and bullshitting in the teacher's lounge. The door was open and he could hear two people talking. He knew it was Russ even before he could see him. That nasally pitched voice pretending to be an expert on everything. Ethan ducked his head as he passed to avoid eye contact. They stopped talking and he wondered if it was due to a lull in their conversation or if they'd indeed made the connection between brown cardboard box and pink slip. Or perhaps Fenske had already opened her mouth about the good news and the rumor

179

mill was already churning. Either way, it made no difference. People would piece things together soon enough.

Something about the word she used – 'terminated' – made it all feel so final, so definite. And it gave Ethan this feeling, this urge, to make his final rounds, to savor his last steps inside Park View Elementary. To get back to the parking lot, to his car, he took the long way around, and before long he found himself standing outside the entrance to the gymnasium.

He opened the double doors and walked inside. The massive space had so much room for life, such prospect for thrill and excitement. He wanted to hear sneakers squeaking, the echo of the ball, the fans. But unlike the students in the hallway just moments before, these sounds were not coming to him as easily. The room was empty. There was no life, only the potential for it. Ethan looked out from the edge of the gym at the empty bleachers, the scoreboard. The room promised so many dreams. Hopes of success and fame, game winning shots, and the ecstasy of being thrust upon the shoulders of peers.

He walked a little further into the gym and on to the corner of the court. The hardwood had a special way of echoing, yet simultaneously swallowing any noise made in the room. He dropped the cardboard box at his feet, and the sound shot out quickly, hit the walls, then came rushing back into the open box, like a well thrown boomerang.

As Ethan knelt down, he pulled his key ring from his belt loop and turned to be sure no one was standing behind him. On the key ring there was a knock-off Swiss Army knife - it had been a gift from his auto insurance company after ten years of customer loyalty…huh, he thought, loyalty - the small one with mini-scissors, a blade, nail file, toothpick and tweezers. He extracted the blade and hovered over the exact right angle where the baseline met the sideline. Jamming the knife into the wood, he carved out three letters:

EMA

His initials. Ethan Michel Atkinson. They were small, half inch by half inch at most, but they were deep, and would not be easily buffed away. They served their purpose.

Since the school day had been cut short, and the building virtually empty, he figured he could extend his stay a while longer and hang out alone in the locker room for a bit. Outside of Pat Bush, the P.E. Teacher, there'd be no reason for anyone to be in there. And since physical education was left off the Parent/Teacher curriculum, Bush actually had a full day's vacation.

Ethan approached a small bench in the middle section of the center aisle, straddled it, and then sat down, putting the box in front of him. He let out a sigh, it was deep and audible, and he rubbed both his neck and forehead, alternating between the two, trying to relieve the mounting tension. The worry was manifesting itself. Details of the morning, the facts, the actuality of what had happened, and they were all beginning to cause a fuss on his insides. His stomach crunched into a ball and his lungs could hardly hold oxygen. Ethan tossed his head back toward the ceiling, wondering how many people over the years had sought refuge from the exact same bench he was sitting on now. Park View had been built in 59', so one a year maybe? Forty, fifty people? How did their stories end?

After a few minutes, and after he felt like he could breathe again, Ethan stood up and walked to the janitor's closet. It felt like a good idea, like the right thing to do, things coming full circle, that sort of thing. Ethan pulled a roll of paper towels from the shelf and wrapped his wrist and fingers several times. Carefully, he removed the cap from a bottle of Ammonia, and poured it into his palm, being sure not to let a drop escape to the floor this time around. He was a professional now. He had experience, and experience breeds confidence. With the towels pressed to his face, he pulled the vapors into the soft inner lining of his nostrils. The drugs knife pierced the front of his brain and he collapsed to the floor. He inhaled again, this time slower, hoping to feel each individual cell as they transformed. For a full minute he was high, he was safe and warm. The load had been lifted. The floor felt like pudding and his bones settled in, becoming one with the pudding, and then he could no longer tell where his legs ended and the floor began.

When the minute was over he turned his head and opened his eyes. Russ was there, standing over him with a look of deep concern and utter disappointment. For once, Russ said nothing. The sight reared his tongue dysfunctional. All he could manage was a bitter, slight, shake of his head.

OCTOBER 20

By this time another cold front had moved in and stopped the sun from shinning so brightly. Where before it had been blue and clear, it was now a chalky grey. Passing cars all had their headlights on, though it was still afternoon. The huff high had been gone for nearly two hours, but the headaches that followed were in full force, and showed no signs of quit. His temples pounded in meter. The throbbing was intense, causing a constant squint-blink action just to relieve the pressure. Ethan didn't mind, it was a reduced sentence as far as he was concerned. He had been driving for hours, in every possible direction, there was no clear destination. Parking lot to parking lot again, and when he'd get to one, he'd decide on another and drive, usually five or ten miles per hour below the speed limit, to the next location. He'd seen Forest Park, midtown, and downtown, cruised Lindbergh Boulevard from

South County to Kirkwood and now, with rush hour traffic starting to build, he found himself driving in circles around the Galleria's parking lot. The low fuel light came on four miles ago; he figured there was another twenty-six in the tank before he had to take the warning seriously.

But he was also avoiding a gas station pit stop. The fumes in the air, lingering from pump nozzles and seeping out of gas caps, would be too strong to resist. Ethan decided that what he'd just done in the school, what Russ had witnessed, would be his last, that he would never again succumb to the urge. He convinced himself that he had willpower within, no matter how small the amount, and he would use it, and build it with positive experiences.

Feel the pounding in your head. Live with who you are, who you've become.

Once out of the parking lot and onto Hanley Road, he began taking notice of the changing neighborhoods, commercial to residential, and wondered how different his life might have been if his grandparents had decided to raise them in a different part of town. The car was silent, all but the engine and the tires spitting pavement below.

How dare Russ pass his bullshit silent judgment on me, he doesn't have a clue what I've been through. Forty-eight years old. Single. And I guarantee he hasn't loved hard enough to fathom what I've lost. Probably a pedophile, anyway.

The miles past quickly as he drove on auto pilot. Ethan was driving on Gravois Road now, headed north again, just past the county cop station. But he couldn't remember exactly how he'd gotten there, what roads he'd taken or specific cars he'd kept pace with along the way. The light up ahead turned yellow and then red. He stopped.

There was a dive cattycorner and the sign on its rooftop advertised brain sandwiches. His grandfather used to boast of the place, of how he never had a problem finishing a sliced and

184

And week after week, for years, he was left unsatisfied. The repeated excuse of *Faith* became a copout.

Above the alter in Salem Lutheran Church, Jesus Christ hung from the cross. It was all there: the crown, the dripping blood, the holes in the hands and feet, the gash in his ribcage. He looked pathetic, helpless. It was a horrific symbol of torture, with his arms cast out, his body drooping. They mounted a crime scene, a homicide! *This is the place we come to be rejuvenated, for our fulfillment?* He often wondered about other martyrs. If the family and friends, the disciples of Martin Luther King Jr., would wear a small Remington Gamemaster Pump Action Rifle around their necks as a symbol of their love and devotion. Did the families of 9-11 victims pin plastic airline wings to their lapels? Surely, he once said to his sister, this must have been a clerical error by early Christian management.

Yet even on this day, sitting in his car, with his life unraveling little by little each day, he found comfort in the cross. He didn't believe a lick of the story, and he wasn't searching for a "savior," but what he was looking for, he found atop the green steeple of Salem Lutheran. History. Family history. The hours upon hours upon years inside that building, sitting next to his sister, his only real family member. Vacation bible school, prayer before meals and bedtime, the constant guilt of today in the name of tomorrow's everlasting life. Christmas! Christmas for Christ's sake! These events battered him with fear, ingrained him with it, and that fear could only be managed by the cross. And now that his foundation had been rocked to the core, with nothing left to salvage, it was only natural that he came to this place, to Salem, the root of his youth, in hopes of clinging onto something, finding some ray of hope, before throwing in the towel altogether.

"Give me a sign," he muttered to the steeple. "Give me a sign." This time he pushed the words past his teeth and through the windshield. The pressure in his temples pressed against the backs of his eyes. "Give me something!" he screamed. Tears broke through and emotion exploded from every pore. He needed an answer, a miracle, something, anything, a bird to drop from the sky, the radio in his car to magically click on, the clouds to part and shine a ray of fucking sunshine onto that god forsaken cross! He would settle for someone to simply open the church door and walk outside, prove to him that there was life inside.

But there was nothing. Nothing happened. There was nothing for him to read into, to project God into. Just the stillness, the quietness he'd become so accustom to. With the engine shut off, the car began to chill, and Ethan could see his breath. He looked up through his windshield, past the steeple, and into the dense, gray sky. The clouds were full and motionless. There was only stillness and his breath.

NOVEMBER 20

"You look ravishing," he said between sips before slowly putting his whiskey glass back on the table. She said nothing but she smiled and tucked a piece of her thick red hair behind her ear, and wondered if he had followed her to the bar or if it *was* just a coincidence, as he'd claimed. "Let's get out of here," he said, shaking his glass to be sure it was empty. "Huh, what do you say? Go back to your place?" He stood up from the table and extended his hand, waiting for her to take it and walk out with him. His stomach was on fire, and despite the warmth and humidity, the stuffiness of a hundred bodies cramped inside the bar, a wave of chills shot up from his lower back and raised the hairs on his neck. The craving was nearly unbearable. He thought of taking her by the shoulders, overpowering her, dragging her outside to the fresh winter air, and there he'd kiss her, with force, make her remember how good it felt the last time they touched. Even if it was a dead fucking end.

"How'd you know I'd be here?" she asked, looking up at him and smiling.

"I didn't."

"I thought you ran away. Disappeared or something."

"I'm right here," he said, waving his arm at her, calling for her to stand up.

"Where you been, Ethan?" There was anger building inside her, he could see it in her shoulders, the way she squared up to him, ready to fight. "You ignore my calls for a month. Avoid me. Now you're here and you want me to take your hand and what? Go back to your place and fuck? Is that gonna fix things here? You drunk? You wanna use me now, cuz I'm here and I'm in front of you?"

"Tammy. Listen to me." Something about his tone completely disarmed her. She sensed honesty, sincerity in his voice. As he looked into her eyes, he lowered his head and grinned like a horny teenager. "I'm not drunk…yet."

She was however, and she rolled her head away and twirled a finger in a strand of red hair until it was fully wrapped. His persistence and charm flattered her, it filled her, and he knew he'd won, he knew he'd have her any way he'd like. "Take my hand. We'll walk out of here together and go back to your place," Ethan said. "I'm sorry I haven't been around or called you back. But I'll explain it. I'll explain it all to you if you just stand up, put your coat on and follow me out of this shitty little bar."

She paused for a moment, staring at him, weighing the truth of his words. Then she said, "You met me in this bar."

"You're right. So maybe it's not that shitty."

Tammy looked around the bar before making a decision. Ethan wondered who or what exactly it was she was looking for, if she was there with someone, her next victim perhaps. Maybe he

190

was in the bathroom and she was sitting here at the table, waiting to seduce him, waiting to watch him tangle himself in her web, struggle, suffer, suffocate, and then, inevitably, give into her. She could proceed to slit his throat and drain his blood, down to the last drop.

"Okay," she said. "I'll forgive you. Take me out of here."

The rush from the cold night's air hitting their lungs was like a rebirth. They could feel breathing. The fresh oxygen made them appreciate how good life could be. But the feeling faded as quickly as it came, and once they were accustomed to the chilly air and breathing normally, their problems and attitudes, life's realities, found focus.

A young couple was approaching the front entrance to The Royale. The girl was running ahead of her man to limit her time out in the cold, but she wore high heels and black leggings so she ran stiff, taking extra care not to slip and fall. On top, she had a thick wool winter jacket, with fur around the hood. Ethan knew that jacket, he knew it well. Maggie had the same one, same color and all. It used to hang in their hall closet. Before any memories could fully rise to the surface he cast them away, choosing instead to think about her near the end, when she was ugly, when she stood in the door with her suitcases packed. Sleet started to fall but it was misty and not terribly bothersome.

"Where are you taking me?" Tammy said. She buttoned her coat to her neck to protect herself from the weather.

"Your place."

She didn't respond with words but her silence was loaded with inquisition. Something was off with Ethan, detached to put it more accurately. He was there in body, with enthusiasm, charm, wit, but his eyes were vacant. Still, something about his absence had drawn her in and aroused her. Tammy was on guard, protective of her own feelings, but nevertheless, she wanted to navigate him, to conquer his lost soul.

191

The moment Tammy entered her apartment she threw her off her shit, piece by piece, letting things fall wherever. Ethan walked in more cautiously, trying to avoid stepping on and breaking something, a plate, hair dryer, the cat. She was gone, disappeared into the bedroom, and Ethan was once again alone among the havoc and destruction.

The happy couples from the phony photos on the walls seemed to be mocking him.

"Why do you have fake pictures in here?"

"They're not fake," she called out.

"They're not you."

"So what."

"So… why don't you have pictures of…your friends?" Ethan adjusted the photo on the wall to straighten it again.

She made a dismissive noise.

"Family then."

Tammy walked out from the darkness of her bedroom and stood in the doorway, leaning most of her weight on her left leg, while her right bent slightly at the knee, and her toes dug and curled into the carpet. She was naked. Her thick red hair was loose and it stopped around her nipples. Her right leg, the bent leg, was swaying back and forth like a sheet hung out on the laundry line in a breezy summer day. It exposed and then covered her vagina repeatedly. The amount of it he saw depended how hard the wind blew. She wasn't trying to be sexy, she was going for blunt, raw. The way she held herself upright, the tone in her eyes, her soft, non-erect nipples. She looked like a naked woman, and nothing more, something from an anatomy text book.

"I was adopted," she said in defense of her photos. "They both died within two years of each other. The pictures I have on my wall are the ones I want on my wall."

Ethan waited a moment, only to allow her seriousness to reach its full effect, and then he said okay. He told her he didn't

192

have a problem with it, or with anything else about her. He said he felt lucky to know her. She turned and walked back, fading into her dark bedroom. Ethan took off his coat and lit the fat candle on top of the massive television. He wasn't sure why he was setting a mood but he did it with a smile on his face, like he had hoped to surprise her. But something about her apartment, the smell of it, the mess of it, maybe the fact that he'd allowed himself to get involved with someone who lived in such a pile of shit, irritated him and made him angry. On one hand, yes, Ethan did want to fuck her, but he also wanted to fight with her. Part of him, more of him maybe, wanted to yell and scream, to get red faced with rage and passion. He wanted to show her how powerful he could be, to scare her, to excite her with danger. And then, if all went well, if he still felt like having her, he'd take her. Maybe against a wall or a window. He wanted to be an animal, to dominate her, and he hoped she would be down to play the little game.

Tammy came out of the room in a night gown. She looked sexy as hell, if only she would just stop and pose for a photo. But it was the way she moved, the way she walked, it was disgusting. She flopped around the apartment, flat footed and sexless, paying no attention to him or the ambiance he'd created. She was a god damn contradiction and it confused Ethan, frustrated him.

"You seem to have lost some of your energy," he said to her.

Tammy was in the kitchen, rooting through the pantry and refrigerator. Ethan couldn't see her but he could hear rummaging. "Yeah. I suppose," she said. "It's nothing. Just being at home, ya know. It can throw my mood." The faucet turned on and he could hear a glass filling. When she walked back into the living room, she moved a few things on the coffee table to make room for her water, set the glass down, and sprawled her legs across the couch. "You know how just being in your own place can relax you. Or depress you."

Ethan nodded. He was leaning with one elbow on the stupid gigantic television.

"And then you started asking questions."

"Questions?"

"Yeah. Questions. The pictures on the wall." Tammy turned her head to look at him and lock eyes. "Makes me feel like you think I'm strange. I mean, I know I'm strange, to the rest of them out there, but I thought you were different. I know you're different. You can see through that other shit. See me. My soul. Like when you first made love to me, I know you could see my soul and I know I could see yours."

Ethan stood tall and started biting the nail on his pinky finger. He had a different recollection of that evening and he wanted to tell her so. But he didn't. He stayed silent.

"So then when you start pointing out different things, things I can tell you don't like about me, or aren't normal to you in your world..." she trailed off. Tears were building in her eyes. "Listen, there are some things I don't like talking about and we'll just leave it at that. You asked me why I got weird and quiet all of a sudden well, that's why. I'm sure there are things you're not jumping to talk to me about either."

Ethan stopped chewing his finger nail and dipped it into the wax puddle inside the fat candle on top of the TV. She was right, some things didn't need prodding, even if it was accidental.

"See, you got shit, too." She sat up a little on the couch, either making room for him or preparing to attack. Ethan couldn't tell. "I could tell by the way you looked away from me right then. I could tell. Like maybe about your ex. What did you say her name was? Maggie?"

Ethan glared at her from the side of his eye, wondering where she was taking him. Wondering if she was setting a trap, or perhaps, if it was too late and he was already standing in it.

194

"Yeah, Maggie. That was it," Tammy said. "You don't like talking about her, do you? It doesn't feel good. We'll, I keep other people on my wall and I don't wanna talk about it either. Okay?"

Ethan nodded.

There was silence, then, "Did you go back to her? Is that why you disappeared?

Ethan looked at her and just shook his head.

"Take your coat off and sit next to me. Tell me where you've been."

He unbuttoned his coat and laid it neatly over the arm of her couch before sitting next to her. "I lost my job. I got fired. I went into hiding for a while. Didn't feel much like leaving my house."

Tammy made the noises girls make, the Ohhhh's and Awww's. Then she rubbed his back, a feeble attempt at comfort, but it worked. Especially when sliding her fingers up and down the skin of his neck. Ethan told her he was fine, that he'd had time to process things, that maybe it would all be for the better in the end, "One door closes and another opens," he mumbled. Eventually Tammy moved her mouth close to his face and began kissing his cheek and eyes, rubbing her nose against his skin and tonguing his ear lobes. It felt nice but it was also wet, and therefore on some level gross and unwanted. He looked down at his pants, his dick was unresponsive.

"Where's your box, your cigar box?" Ethan asked. He was kissing her back now, returning the affection, but only to appease.

"The H?" she said, slightly surprised. She thought that might've been what he was after in the first place, this whole charade, tracking her at the bar, the sweet talk, the candle. But she wasn't ready to quit on herself. She hoped he still wanted more, wanted her. "Baby, you gotta be careful. I don't' play that often."

195

Ethan held her eyes, challenging her, begging her, and she could tell he needed something other than what she could offer physically. So she leaned in and kissed him, holding on to his bottom lip for an extra beat, before standing to retrieve the box.

When she sat down and opened it, he told her he wanted to do it to her, liked she'd done him. That the experience was so intimate, so sensual, that he wanted her to feel everything she'd given him the last time. As he said these things to her, Ethan was moving his hand up her leg, and heading to the spot she had shown him on her inner thigh, the 'highway'. Tammy smiled and agreed. Her chest was flush and her lips were full from arousal. She felt wanted.

As she lay there, draped across the couch cushions, Ethan guided her night gown over her knees, pushing the fabric together inch by inch, past her thighs, then her ass, and resting the rolled up gown on her stomach. She was completely exposed. She opened herself further, wrapping a leg over Ethan's waist to give him full access to the bruised marking on her leg.

Ethan injected her. Tammy's head sunk into the pillow and her arm fell from her side and hung off the couch. Ethan unwrapped her leg from his lap and tossed the syringe on the coffee table with the rest of the trash. He took a large drink from her glass of water and set it back in its same spot, the same condensation ring. She was sound in her heroine sleep and would be for a good while.

Ethan got up and walked around the apartment, picking up the obvious trash from the coffee table and floor (junk mail, empty soda cans, and the like), and when his hands were full he tossed it all in the wastebasket. Her fridge was sparse, only ketchup, spray butter, and a half empty re-corked bottle of white zinfandel inside. It was sad and disgusting. Tammy's bedroom was clean, comparatively speaking. The bed was made, which struck Ethan as odd, and there was hardly anything on the floor, other than a brush and blow-dryer. The closet, however, was another story. It looked like the rest of the house. Clothes were piled three feet high and the sliding glass door, which was also a full length mirror, was off its rail and hanging askew. There was nothing interesting in her bedroom, at least not on the surface, and Ethan didn't care enough to dig much deeper. He wanted to soak in her atmosphere, to feel what she felt when she walked around the apartment, getting ready for the day, or preparing to end it. He thought about living with her, hypothetically, and what that would be like - the fights they'd have, where he'd put his dresser, whether she capped the toothpaste or left it sitting open all night, oozing and then hardening.

Back in the living room, Ethan stood over her, watching her high. He was jealous, but he also judged her, deemed her a junkie, too pathetic for his tastes. *What would grandma say about this one?* Ethan sat on the corner of the coffee table, and put his face close to hers. He turned his head and put his ear to her lips, listening to her breathe. Ethan reached behind him and grabbed the syringe from the table. He held it in both hands, examining the hypodermic needle, its sharpness, the lumen at the beveled tip, where the medication would spew out. Then he took his t-shirt and wiped the syringe in all the spots he'd been handling it. When he felt it was clean, he took her hand, the hand that was hanging off the couch, and covered the plastic barrel of the syringe with all the prints of her fingers, and pressed her thumb against the butt of the plunger. When he felt it was clear that she was its sole operator, he set the syringe on the carpet, just beneath her hand.

Ethan stood up, took the pillow from the opposite end of the couch, and held it over Tammy's face, pressing the cushion as hard as he could against her ears. After thirty seconds, he bent down close and held the side of his face to the pillow. Ethan smiled to suppress the swelling tears. Ethan was feeling a strange compassion, a strong desire to bring her comfort, to end her

197

struggle. She fought briefly, but she was high and weak. And when she stopped fighting, Ethan held the pillow in place still awhile longer, to be sure. The candle on top of the television flickered, casting shadows up and down the walls. The room was still and quiet. The way he liked it. He could hear the popping of the wick and the fire and the wax. Ethan used his shoulder to wipe a tear from his eye, and then he put the pillow back at the end of the couch, below her cold feet.

Ethan retraced his steps, calmly, slowly, and proceeded to wipe anything he touched with the bottom of his t-shirt: the glass of water, refrigerator door, the framed photos on the wall. When he finished, he took his neatly folded coat off the arm of the couch and closed it, preparing for the cold sleet outside.

"Good night, Tammy." He leaned down and kissed her forehead.

Ethan opened the door with the sleeve of his jacket, and closed it just the same.

•

When he returned home it was nearly midnight, still early, cars were bustling up and down Kingshighway, and he could hear and see them from the living room windows. Ethan was still standing with his back to the door. He needed to be still, he needed the stillness of his home.

He was breathing but the depths of his breaths were shallow, like he was playing dead and any movement might give him away. Finally, when he was calm and could no longer feel his pulse beating against his neck, Ethan turned the deadbolt and chain. He allowed himself to breathe fully, deeply, audibly even. He undid his coat and opened the closet door.

Everything crushed him at once, all that he had managed to burry for weeks and weeks. Maggie's coat was gone. The grey wool winter coat with the fur around the hood, the same one worn by the young girl at the bar. She'd taken it months ago when she'd left, but he noticed now. The goddamn wool coat would hang in the hall closet and not bother a soul. It hung between her rain coat, which was also gone, and his leather jacket. Ethan wanted to smell it, to smell Maggie, to bury his face in the fur that would cover her soft blonde head. There was an empty clarity to everything, the entire duplex looked vacant, Maggie left holes on every wall and in every corner.

The closet was small, three feet by four feet, and the floor was cold. Ethan curled up in one of its corners, running his fingers against the bottom of his leather coat. He wondered if his jacket had fallen in love with hers, if its heart had been impaled when one day it woke to find its companion had suddenly disappeared. Did it miss the fabric? Did it miss its warmth? The color? Ethan stood and searched his leather jacket for one last strand of Maggie's blonde hair. One that maybe slept on the shoulder of her grey wool winter coat, and when the coat was yanked from its home, from its partner, perhaps that last remaining hair caught the collar of Ethan's leather jacket, and it sat there, waiting for him to find it and worship it, to kiss it and care for it. He could find no such hair. There was nothing. Even the cedar hanger contributed to the complete removal of everything Maggie, absorbing whatever scent her grey wool winter coat may have left behind.

There was a box back in the deepest corner of the closet, storage. Ethan reached his hand inside the box, trying to remember the things it might contain. On top was a picture frame, he pulled it out. Ethan's face hardened. The picture frame, the photo inside, was a moment from their first weekend away together, the two of them smiling together, seemingly forever. Ethan had known this photo well, and he had purposely buried it in the furthest corner of the closet so as not to have to see it as regularly as before. It was the old photo from his desk at Park View Elementary, the one that left the vacant hole in his year.

NOVEMBER 24

Three days had passed before anyone found her. It was the landlord, an older woman who lived across the hall from her; she noticed the mail growing in Tammy's box and heard the cat meowing and clawing behind the door. The authorities took the body away for toxicology and conducted a brief but formal investigation. The Post-Dispatch wrote about it on the fourth day.

> A 28-year-old St. Louis woman died Saturday morning of a suspected drug overdose, according to St. Louis Police Chief Rich Parker. She is the third suspicious death of a local young person in the past two months.

Tammy Soleski was discovered in the living room of her home in the 3100 block of Iowa St., Parker said.

Pending autopsy results, Police are treating the death as an accidental overdose because of "paraphernalia" found at the scene, and no other evidence could be found for why someone her age, and in good health, would have died, Parker said.

Authorities have had a difficult time tracking down family and friends of Soleski. She had been adopted as a child and both parents are since deceased.

No visitation time has been scheduled.

Authorities are awaiting toxicology results to confirm the cause of death, which could take up to six weeks. Parker could not say for sure what drugs may have been involved until these results are released, but he said "all signs point to heroin"; a drug that is quickly becoming a major problem for the city and counties of St. Louis.

This death follows an increase in reported overdose deaths in St. Louis City and St. Louis County. The county coroner's office reported a 67% increase in overdose deaths over the past 3 years. Last year, heroin was responsible for 50 deaths in St. Louis County, according to St. Louis County Police Department. This year, there were 49 heroin deaths by the end of June, leading local law enforcement to believe this year's number will soar significantly past 50. The average age range of the victims is between 25 and 30, though there have been a growing number of suburban teenage deaths.

"This problem is reaching into the suburbs," said St. Louis County Police Chief Ron Grier. "It's not a race problem, it's just simply a problem. A big problem."

Heroin, a physically and emotionally addictive depressant, is a major problem in the outlying counties, said Grier.

"The drug is cheap," Grier said, "and at $10 per 1/20 of a gram, a person can get a four-hour high from heroin cheaper than the cost of a six pack of beer." Many people who abuse prescription drugs, which can be expensive, have moved to heroin because the price is so much more affordable.

To determine if your child is using heroin, Parker said signs to look for are: missing cash, checks and valuables, missing or burnt spoons, interaction with new friends, and academic and behavior issues at school. Physical symptoms may include: bloodshot eyes, small pupils, and a discontinued interest in personal hygiene.

"You can do everything right and this can still happen to your child," Parker said.

For help or information in regards to Tammy Soleski, or for help with an addict or to report any information related to heroin users or dealers, officials said to contact the St. Louis City Drug Task Force.

Ethan folded the newspaper in half and then in half again, and set it off to the side of the table, near the salt and pepper shakers and then Heinz 57 ketchup bottle. His heart slowed to a heavy but regular thump. There was a deep exhale as the tension he'd been holding the past weekend was finally relieved, at least temporarily. Ethan looked out the diner window at the passing traffic. The Monday morning commuters were filling Kingshighway. The sun was rising and it was bright in the clear blue sky. Even from inside he could tell the air was crisp; a gorgeous autumn day, leaves were surely falling from the oaks in Tower Grove Park. A perfect morning for a run, he thought. He'd been given a gift. A chance to start anew. No wives or girlfriends, no jobs or children to look after. Square One. A blank slate, a fresh start. Maybe a real move, an actual geographic change, was in order, Chicago perhaps. Still Midwestern but also a big city, somewhere he could get lost in a crowd, blend into the fabric of the city. But he'd have to wait a while. A jump to a new state might raise suspicions if the investigators come calling.

"More coffee, sir?"

The waitress was young, mid-twenties, with acne scars below her cheekbones, and no makeup. She worked in a diner, that was her life. She did not care to impress. Ethan nodded and she filled his cup. As she poured he looked at the name tag on her chest: Josie. She set the coffee pot on the table, next to his Post-Dispatch, and pulled an order pad from the pouch on her apron.

"What are we havin' this mornin'? Slinger?"

"Jesus. No, thank you." Ethan frowned. "I'm gonna keep it simple. Just two eggs, scrambled with cheese."

"What kind?"

"American is fine. And a side of bacon."

"White or wheat?"

"Wheat, please."

Josie picked up the pot and started to walk away.

"You know what?" Ethan said, stopping her. She looked at him for the first time, cocking her head in a way that said 'better make it quick.' "Instead of toast, can I get a pancake on the side?"

"One or two?"

"One is fine."

Josie didn't write the change on the pad. She just walked back behind the counter, checking on the few other customers along the way.

Ethan unpeeled the lid of the plastic coffee creamer and emptied it into his mug. The color changed from black to light brown as he stirred. When he set the spoon in the saucer, the metal on porcelain made a clanging noise and the coffee left on the spoon seeped to the bottom of the saucer, attaching itself to the base of the mug. The grill sizzled when the short-order cook flipped the bacon. The register rang and banged, the check was stabbed, pierced right through its center. The bell rattled against the door and everyone knew someone had either come or gone. A fat man with paint stains on his jeans dropped a quarter into the juke box. A record played. Country. Old with twang. Ethan looked over his shoulder and watched the fat man sit down in his booth. Then he looked out the window again. The sun was higher and brighter. The cars were backing up in both directions.

Ethan stared at the front page of the newspaper, wondering how long until they were on to him. Somewhere between a couple days and the rest of his life, he figured. A life sentence, full of waiting and wondering. Waiting and wondering. And always looking over his shoulder. Chicago didn't seem like such a bad idea after all.

He ate, took his newspaper, paid his tab, and headed a few blocks north toward the park, where it was quiet. Ethan walked through the grass of Tower Grove Park, among the trees, crunching the dried and fallen leaves with each step. A few dogs and their owners were gathered off to the side and away from the main road, in an area of their own, next to the grass tennis courts. They were bundled up in their perfect fleece wear, laughing and making dinner plans or play dates, agreeing on politics, and complementing themselves and each other as often as possible.

The bench where he had first seen Tammy, reading page after page of her novel, and then suddenly caught between a pack of wild playful dogs, was empty. He sat in the same spot she had occupied months before, and he watched with glee, like a jubilant toddler, as the dogs ran free around the bench. Tammy was there, sitting right next to him, buried on page A7 of the Post with a caption and a few words about her death; it was all there for everyone to read. Yet, it seemed so few people knew anything about her life.

NOVEMBER 26

He always calls back. Always. It was remarkably out of character for him not to return his only sister's calls, especially after multiple, semi-urgent messages. Especially regarding their holiday plans, especially Thanksgiving Dinner. She was trying not to get worked up, for the baby's sake as well as her own, but she was losing patience and beginning to worry, and if she worried, Winslow would worry, and then there would be a mess.

Winslow had been keeping a watchful eye since the first signs of her belly taking shape. He was constantly monitoring her every move and mood around the clock. Rachel had gone to great lengths to keep him from over reacting on multiple occasions, most recently while shopping for the essentials at Schnucks. Winslow snapped at the grocery store stock boy for allowing her, a pregnant woman, to reach up on her own to the top shelf for a box of cereal.

He asked for the manager, wanted to write a formal complaint and send it to corporate, he threatened to buy milk elsewhere, somewhere where the employees respected the sanctity of life. His caution and sensitivity were sweet but they were also irrational, and to Rachel, intolerable. After all, she was hormonal and therefore cantankerous.

But this was a different situation altogether. If Winslow began to worry about Ethan, Rachel's fears might take root, become real, and take a firm grip, crippling her decision making capabilities. It might crush her strength. The less either of them knew the better. But for Rachel, it was too late. Inside, she already knew.

There was something eternal between her and her brother, an unequivocal bond that can only be built with history and experience, and blood. But it was thicker than blood and it was being threatened. She could feel it in her bones, in her belly, in her nerves. The warning sirens had been sounding for far too long.

Around two in the morning the frustration and doubt became unbearable, and she could no longer pretend to sleep. Rachel sat up in bed and threw the covers off her legs.

"You okay?" Winslow asked.

"Fine, baby. Just need a glass of water." She lied. But as the words came out she thought that maybe the water might help, might give her a clearer perspective and wash away her nervous stomach, at least until morning.

In the bathroom, the water from the tap was warm against her fingertips, the way she'd preferred it during her pregnancy. They kept a glass on the counter next to the sink and she filled it half way, then finished it in two large swallows. When she looked in the mirror, she could see her hair draping down and framing her face, the whites of her eyes popping in the night. She touched her cheek, and the diamond in her wedding ring showed its reflection. Rachel moved her hand down to her stomach. She felt its shape,

208

the way it curved and molded to her hips like the contours of a porcelain vase. But she was cold inside, empty. She heard the warning sounding again, this time in her temples, and in her joints.

Downstairs, she quietly threw on her coat, and escaped the house through the kitchen sliding glass door. Rachel drove to her brother's duplex on the south side of the park. From her car she could see that his lights were on, at least in the living room, but his blinds were closed and there was no visible movement on the other side. She parked the car across the street and got out. The walkway to the duplex had a guide rail flanking the stairs, but the wrought iron had rust at its base and was unsteady as a result, and could barely support her weight.

Rachel's pulse was racing as she approached his front entry. Worse case scenarios played out in her mind. She worried where Ethan might be if he weren't home. She worried what she might find if he was. She worried what affect her anxiety was having on the tiny thing growing inside her stomach.

Rachel rang the doorbell.

There was no answer. But she could hear music, a base drum coming from the top of the stairs.

She rang the doorbell again, holding the button longer this time, hoping to jar him awake, hoping he was only asleep.

Again, there was no answer.

Rachel dug into her coat pocket for her key ring and located the spare Maggie had given her in case of emergencies or a lockout. Without hesitation she jammed the key into the door knob and let herself in. She rushed up the narrow staircase as quickly as her body would allow. The faster she moved, the less time she had to think, to second guess and blame. No matter how terrible the images passing through her head might have seemed, she refused to submit, she refused to panic. For the babies sake. At her age, she knew she had to be careful. It wasn't likely that she'd get a second chance.

Rachel muttered curse words as she climbed the stairs, most of them directed inward. She was angry for not being there for her brother, for not being more concerned and available. He needed her, clearly, and she had been selfishly consumed with her own happiness, wanting to enjoy her own life, her own home, her own husband, and preparing for *their* child. And while it was comforting to care for her brother, to be the mother he never had (and the sister and the best friend), to be his foundation, if she continued to be responsible, to feel an obligation to his well-being, she'd continue to live in the past. And the past was just that, past. Gone. She was ready to bury it forever. Winslow helped provide that illusion. He made her feel like she was normal, like she came from someplace that was not all that dissimilar from every other person on the planet. He grounded her.

But in the end that's all it was, an illusion. It would be impossible for her to live any other life. Ethan was part of that past, a constant reminder of the life that was thrust upon her. There was no way to completely sever ties, it just wasn't that simple, it wasn't black and white. She wanted desperately to detach her present life from the youth that shaped her. But she lived her life in the gray, caught between who she'd become and who she'd escaped.

When she reached the top stair, she tried to recall when it was she last saw her brother. Nearly a month must have passed, she thought. And the family dinners, which used to be so regular, had whittled away shortly after Maggie had the abortion. The cemetery: that was the last time they'd spoken to one another. As momentous as that scene now felt, at nearly three o'clock in the morning, on the verge of a nervous breakdown, she'd spent the past four weeks downplaying the entire event. He was drunk. He was tired. He was mad at mom, nothing more. When she retold the story to Winslow, she left out sections, smoothing it over, making everything that was so brutal and painful seem mundane, as though pissing on his mother's grave was commonplace, nothing truly out of the ordinary. Rachel cursed herself again. Why, she wondered, did she wait so long to take action? He was crying out for help in his own way and she dismissed everything. She didn't want to admit that Ethan might have a problem too heavy to handle on his own, too heavy even for her. Plus, she was tired of being her brother's keeper. She wanted only to be Rachel, Winslow's Rachel.

The music she'd heard on his front porch was louder now and leaking out from beneath the door. A good and positive sign, she told herself. She knocked and pressed her ear against the door, hoping to hear movement or footsteps on the other side, a party, a one night stand, anything.

Rachel used the spare again. As she opened the door, a strong rush of adrenaline blast out from her kidney and everything was vivid. The colors of the room were bright and the music sharp. The record player was spinning and she could hear and see the needle grinding against the vinyl. A specific and familiar anxiety slammed against the bottom of her stomach before exploding throughout the rest of her body.

For the first time in the course of her pregnancy she felt her child kick. He was tumbling around inside her.

Rachel covered her mouth and nose to block the smell of Ethan's home. There were days, maybe even weeks' worth of fast food trash littering the entire room. French fries and soda cups sat unfinished on the couch. Crumbled McDonalds bags were lying next to Jack in the Box taco wrappers. There were beer cans, beer bottles, and empty pints of liquor. Dishes were piling in the sink and trash overflowing in the can. It reeked of depression. And gasoline.

On the floor, beneath the coffee table, she could see her brother's legs. They were motionless and naked. He wore only a t-shirt and white briefs. Rachel took it all like a right hook across

211

the jaw. It buckled her knees and nearly knocked her down. She pressed her back against the wall to keep from falling.

Déjà vu. The bitter past that she tried so hard to forget had resurfaced. That specific anxious feeling was familiar because she'd known it well, as a child. One explicit memory seemed to come to life and coexist with reality. It was distinct and brilliant. And its likeness was as real and vibrant as the sights and sounds and smells of her brother's duplex.

She was suddenly pummeled by a memory. Twelve years old. Walking home from school, backpack tight against her spine. She could hear the spring action screen door slam behind her as she walked into the house. The sun emptied itself into the kitchen, casting shadows and sharp beams of light from the window above the sink to the table where, together with their father, she and Ethan would eat breakfast each morning. But something was different, something was off. The house was calm, void of sound and life. Rachel knew something was off, wrong from the moment the latch on the screen door caught. She felt alone. In the center of the kitchen she stopped and stood quietly, watching specks of dust dance in the sunlight, waiting for something to instruct her next move. She tried to listen to the sounds of the house but her ears felt like they had been covered. There was no sound at all, just a vacant, hallow emptiness, like listening to a seashell.

"Daddy?" she called out. Even her own voice felt trapped inside her head. "Daddy?" she said even louder.

Rachel walked down the long hallway just off the kitchen, toward her and Ethan's bedroom. The door was closed. She cracked it open and stuck her head inside, weary of what she might find. Several toy cars were spread out on the carpet. Her brother was asleep on the bottom bunk.

She closed the door and continued down the hall to her father's room, the one he used to share with their mother. She walked the hallway with caution, one slow step at a time, the loud calls for her father turning into a soft whisper, "Daddy...Daddy..."

When she got to the room, she noticed the bed was neatly made and an envelope had been propped up against the pillows. On the floor just outside the closet, she saw the dining room chair lying on its side. Rachel's twelve year old eyes followed the body of the chair into the closet, its four legs pointing out into the bedroom, its flat seat in the doorway leading inside to the beveled engraving on its back. Her tiny feet took several steps further into the room. There was a hammer on the closet floor and some chunks of plaster. She could see her father's toes suspending in midair. His jeans. His slumping head. The orange electrical cord, the one he used to keep rolled up out in the garage, was tied in a knot between two holes in the ceiling, and attached to his neck. He had hanged himself. With his six year old son sleeping in the next room. And he left his daughter, still a child herself, to clean up the mess. Both parents gone in just a handful of years.

Rachel yanked her brother from his bunk and sprinted to the grass in the backyard where they cried together for nearly an hour before a neighbor finally heard their tears and came to rescue them.

●

The baby kicked hard. Rachel's mouth was dry and her hands were shaking. As she stared at Ethan, lying motionless on the floor, years of pent up hatred toward her father began to resurface. Such a small, small man, she thought to herself. She could see his face in her mind's eye, a high school photo her grandmother kept on a wall. A coward of a man, John Atkinson. It was an embarrassment, Rachel thought, to share his name for so many years. He was a wart, taking the low road like that, leaving his two children parentless, loveless. To abandon them! What kind

213

of example was he trying to set? Who did he think would find him, hanging there? Fucking asshole! Love lost does not have to mean life lost.

It clicked for Rachel the moment the first shovelful of dirt hit the top of his casket. Her father hated Ethan, blamed him for their mother's death, considered him a murderer.

Rachel wiped a stream of tears from her cheek with the back of her hand. With clear eyes she surveyed the room, taking deep breaths to regain composure. There was an open suitcase packed with clothing on the floor just outside the bedroom, and the coffee table was covered with boxes and photos. But the smell of gasoline was still strong.

She fell from the wall down to her brother's feet and pulled at his t-shirt, dragging him out from beneath the table. His body was limp. A bottle of whiskey spilt from his right hand and stained the carpet, in the left hand he still held the rag, soaked in gasoline. The muscles in Rachel's stomach clinched and quivered. She tore the rag from his hand and grabbed his face, squeezing his skin and screaming, begging him to open his eyes.

"Wake up! You're not done here, Ethan! Wake up!"

In anger, in desperation, she slapped his face repeatedly until his skin turned red with the outlines of her fingers. A moan escaped from his lips. It was small but it was audible. Rachel peeled back his eyelids and there was movement. There was still some life inside. Relief consumed her. She pulled her brother's head into her lap and brushed the hair from his eyes. Tears rushed out from behind her own eyes, and with her face hovering over his, they landed on Ethan. Rachel took her free hand and grabbed Ethan's wrist, laying his open palm on her pregnant belly.

"Uncle Ethan, stay with me," Rachel said, trying to smile through the tears. "There is someone here who needs to meet you."

DECEMBER 14

The muscles in Ethan's forearm were cramping from wrist to elbow as he worked the damp rag against the carpet. The elastic band that held the cheap white construction mask tight against his face was pulling and tugging on a section of hair above each of his ears, and inside the mask, sweat droplets had started forming on his lips. But there was no way around it, the place needed a deep cleaning and the fumes had to be kept out of his system. He scrubbed, back and forth, foam building and then soaking into the carpet fibers until the whiskey stain faded and gave way to the carpet's natural egg shell coloring.

Ethan tossed the wet rag in the bucket, moved the mask from his mouth to his forehead, and sat back on his heels to take a breather. Excluding the few nail holes marking the spots where his things once hung, the walls were naked, bare, white, and the remaining furniture, what they couldn't sell, was stacked and packed with other storage in the back of Rachel and Winslow's garage. Thoughts and memories from years of living there, scenes that took place inside the duplex – his time in college when it was his bachelor pad, then his life with Maggie, his happy life, watching movies, drinking wine with his sister and brother in law till all hours of the morning – were beginning to replay themselves. He tried to fight them off but there were too many, and together they were overpowering. But they were mostly happy and they reminded him of a life he used live.

Without his personality decorating each room – pictures, books, tables and chairs, the old record player, the couch, the pillows and blankets, all the color that once surrounded him – the duplex just looked old, like every other brick building neighboring the park. It looked exactly like it had when his landlord handed him the keys eight years earlier. Yet, somehow, he was no longer taken by its architectural charms, they were lost on him. The French doors leading outside to the balcony were drafty and out of date. And the balcony itself in some way felt unsafe, like the wood floor was rotting with termites, and the brick columns framing the corners looked as though the mortar was weathered and crumbling to dust. Inside the plumbing was loud, the stove too small, and the crown molding was loosening and showing gaps in the corners of the ceiling. The character lacked character.

But he had made love on the living room carpet, many times, he thought as he ran his fingers across it, and there were many rainy April weekends when he and Maggie would take turns playing records (The Beatles, Simon and Garfunkel, Karen Dalton, Otis Redding) while looking through those French doors and watching raindrops bounce off the green leaves of the sycamore across the street in Tower Grove. This was the place that he called home for nearly a decade. It was the duplex that accepted him, that

216

allowed him to drop his guard and exist free of judgment and discrimination. It was in this duplex that he could just exist.

Ethan was no longer angry at Maggie. The past few weeks had shown him the value in staying mad. There was none. The past few weeks had also shown him the consequences of continuing to harbor anger. There were many. Ethan decided to forgive her and move on. He called to tell her so, and also apologize for his own behavior, the way he'd alienated himself and vilified the one person he'd ever truly loved. She thanked him and apologized for hurting him too, explaining how her actions had not been carefully thought out, that she understood she'd violated trust boundaries, but that she was also hurt, still hurting actually, and hearing his voice on the other line was more contact than she could handle. She just simply wasn't ready, hadn't healed. There were several uncomfortable eternity seconds of silence. Then they hung up and continued on their separate ways. Too much had happened and it changed each of them, for better or worse. They went into it together, and when they came out on the other side, they were different people, distant people. The relationship had run its course.

Rachel was peeling yellow rubber gloves off her hands when she walked out of Ethan's bedroom. She had a light green bandana tied around her head to keep the hair off her face, and her belly pressed against her paint stained t-shirt. But she was beautiful, radiant. The glow was back and it followed her wherever she went. It was bright and magical, like dancing butterflies, or a glittering halo. There was nothing she could do to hide it, and that specific mother-to-be glow made Ethan smile. He was proud of the life Rachel created, that she'd found such happiness with Winslow. Ethan knew firsthand how great a mother she would be; a perfect mother, full of love and affection, caring, but also stern and direct. A perfect blend. She used those same qualities to raise him.

"What time is it?" she said.

Ethan dried his hands on the carpet and pulled his phone from his pocket. "Quarter till."

"You should get cleaned up. Wins will be here soon."

Ethan stood and walked to the kitchen. He'd packed a change of clothes in a duffle bag earlier and left it on the counter.

"There's a little touch up left to do on the wall," Rachel said. "I guess from the head board. Nice work." She raised a mischievous and knowing eyebrow.

Ethan shook his head while washing his hands in the kitchen sink. Her mind was almost as dirty as her mouth and neither one ceased to amaze him. When he was just ten, and she sixteen, Rachel had taught him about the birds and the bees and how to most effectively use his stinger. He later found out she was in college before she lost her virginity and all her "knowledge" had come from perusing Cosmopolitan magazines at the grocery store, and sneaking off to the basement with copies of their grandmother's trashy romance novels.

Rachel reached into the Home Depot bag on the floor and removed the plastic wrapping from a paint brush. "I'll finish it up while you guys are gone. I wanna get out of here before dinner."

Ethan looked at her with admiration. She was a strong woman, strong enough to keep both their heads above water no matter how large the storm. "You have too much energy for a pregnant woman," he said, drying his hands on his jeans.

"Shit, boy. There's work to be done and daylight's runnin' out." Rachel walked across the room and opened the French doors. "Need some air in here. It's warm." She walked out to the balcony, took in a deep breath of cold, fresh air, and stepped back inside. "How's the carpet?" she asked.

"Like new. Came up easier than I thought, actually."

"Good. You should hop in the shower, seriously, he's gonna be here and I don't wanna deal with him if you guys are late."

"He's always late," Ethan said, grabbing the duffle. "What are you talking about?"

"Not for meetings. Never." Rachel leaned against the door catching the cold breeze as it first entered. "Hey, don't make a mess in there. I'm not cleaning that damn tub again. And wipe down the sink."

"Motherhood suits you," Ethan said with pointed cynicism.

Rachel gave him the finger.

He stopped on his way to shower and looked at his sister, the bare trees in the park just over her shoulder in the background, the doors framing her profile as she looked out into the gray winter day with her hands on her stomach. A beautiful photo, if only he had a camera. He stood there, staring at her, taking the picture in his head, wanting to savor the moment so that one day, forty or fifty years down the road, he could remember this image of her and how she'd been the one to come to his rescue. She was an angel. She saved him. Ethan walked to her, kissed her cheek, and wrapped her in his arms. "Thank you," he said softly into her ear. "Thank you."

"Of course. You're my baby brother." At first Rachel thought he was referring to her help with the move, with cleaning and painting, but as he held her and pulled her tightly into his chest, she realized what it was exactly he was thanking her for, that it was for everything, for a lifetime. Rachel could feel her eyes starting to water.

The front door opened, interrupting them, breaking the embrace. Winslow barged in with a tray full of coffee in one hand and a grocery bag in the other. His energy was frantic, like he'd purchased a separate tray of coffee for himself and drank that one on the way over. But it was probably nothing more than the rush of the day – the parking, the cold weather, a pregnant wife, trying to climb Ethan's rickety staircase without spilling half a cup of scolding hot java down his wrist. Winslow set the tray on the counter and started warming his hands by rubbing them together. "I got two tall venti something-or-others, the vacuum is still in the trunk, trash bags are in here," Winslow said as he emptied the contents of the grocery bag. "And last but most importantly, a pint of Ben and Jerry's Chunky Monkey for my queen." He was grinning wide, nothing but white teeth and big gums. Winslow was still a boy, still full of youthful exuberance. As he presented the ice cream, he noticed Ethan and Rachel standing side by side. They were less emotional than the moment before. His presence had made them cheery, and they welcomed his unique enthusiasm for life into their day. "Look at you, not even showered! What are you doing?" Winslow pulled the sleeve of his jacket over his wrist and checked his watch. "It's five till."

"Your clock's fast."

"Whatever, man. Let's roll."

"Let me rinse off." Ethan said, kissing his sisters head once more. "Count to thirty, I'll be out before thirty-one."

"One, two, three, four…"

Ethan left them alone in the empty living room and moved for the shower. Winslow, who had stopped counting once Ethan left the room, felt a gust creep in from the balcony. He abruptly put his coffee on the counter and rushed across the room, shaking his head with every step.

"You two have the same crazy blood flowing through your veins, that's for sure," he said, as he closed the French doors.

•

Ethan stood in front of the sink, losing himself in the mirror, drifting through sections of his face – a chunk of his pupil, the dark freckle to the left of his nose, the way the hairs on his face grew thick and straight in spots but failed to grow at all in others – until the bathroom filled with steam from the shower, and his face disappeared entirely. These days, that's how he would know that the water was ready. It needed to be hot, scalding. When the water hit his flesh he wanted his skin to turn red, he wanted to sweat. He would hang his head under the shower head and let the heat pound against his neck, creating a waterfall above his eyebrows and down his face. And when one spot burned and became too much to handle, he'd turn sideways, cook his shoulder for a few minutes, and turn again, letting the water change the color of his chest. In Ethan's mind, it was a way to cleanse himself both inside and out. He'd developed a routine: wait for the water to heat up, rotate in the heat like he was on a rotisserie, and then, before washing with soap and washcloth, he'd spend several minutes thinking about Tammy.

Every day since he'd last seen her, since he held the couch pillow over her mouth and suffocated her to death, he would think about her while he was in the shower. And that was the only time he thought of her. At no other point throughout his day did Tammy ever cross his mind, not even the slightest recollection penetrated his thoughts. Out of sight, out of mind. Her death brought not only an obvious physical end to their relations, but also a total non-existence, as if nothing ever happened. Because he was either scared or embarrassed, Ethan had never once brought Tammy up in conversation with Rachel or Winslow, and since he lost his job, there was no interaction with friends or co-workers, no one to converse with on any topic, really. So the only person he had ever even talked to about Tammy, was Tammy. And since he killed her, talking to her was no longer an option.

Ethan had done an excellent job of blocking out everything, of moving on and starting fresh. He'd convinced himself, Rachel, Winslow, and a team of doctors running the Barnes-Jewish Hospital Chemical Dependency Program that he was in recovery, that the night Rachel found him huffing unleaded gasoline under his coffee table was actually rock bottom, that he'd never thought of suicide, and that he'd never truly indented to harm himself, and most certainly not anyone else.

And yet, there in the shower, he was unable to escape the simple truth. Ethan Atkinson had gotten away with murder. The authorities had all but closed the case before they left Tammy's apartment; accidental heroin overdose, no family to notify, only a few friends to even attend a funeral, and one unfortunate little old slum-lord-land-lady to find a cold dead body. Sure, the lead detective on Tammy's case had visited Ethan. But he was recovering in a white room on the fourth floor of Barnes-Jewish Plaza, and the investigation was nothing more than a formality. The detective said there were witnesses that had claimed to see him and Tammy together, several months before she was found dead. The detective wanted to know if Ethan had any information. He didn't. The detective wanted to know if Ethan was aware that Tammy had passed. He wasn't. The detective wanted to know when it was Ethan had last seen or heard from Tammy. He said they'd dated briefly, but that it was merely a fling, a rebound after the breakup with his fiancé, and he'd called it off months ago when he first found out that she was a doper. Ethan explained that he was having a hard enough time battling addiction on his own, and after losing his job and his fiancé, he couldn't be around a substance as hard as heroin. He was good. Smart. Sincere. Believable. The detective gave Ethan her card, said that if he had any information about a dealer or where Tammy might have been getting her supply, that he should call. The detective said they intended to catch the bad guys who were bringing these awful

222

drugs to the streets, and killing innocent people like Tammy Soleski. Ethan asked her what had happened to Tammy's cat. She said it must have escaped with all the commotion, in and out of the apartment. Then the detective left.

Four days later there was a follow up article in the St. Louis Post Dispatch regarding Tammy's death. Accidental Overdose. The article went on to explain how horrific heroin was, that parents should monitor their teens, that the Mexican cartels were dangerous, and the number of OD's and drug related hospitalizations in recent months showed that they were bringing the terrifyingly addictive drug into the suburbs of Missouri and Illinois.

It was burning. He turned a quarter-step in the shower and watched as his chest quickly turned red in the spots where the water landed. The psychological symbolism was obvious even to Ethan, he'd learned as much in his sophomore psych class. The shower was not an unlikely place for him to think of his past sins. He wanted to wash away what he'd done, to forgive himself, to come clean with the truth. But that was not an option, not if he wanted to keep his sister, not if he wanted to be Uncle Ethan, and most certainly not if he had any hopes of ever rekindling things with Maggie, or starting something new and even more beautiful with the next Maggie, whomever she may be.

No, Ethan would have to accept that Tammy would continue to haunt him until the day he joined her, and that he was fortunate she only appeared when she did, when he was alone with his thoughts and his body, beneath the burning water. The sickest part of all, he thought to himself as he replayed her last moments – when her legs squirmed and twitched, and her arms fought to free themselves from beneath the heavy pressure of his knees – was that he may have actually been able to love Tammy, if he would have allowed himself, if he'd have given her a chance at his heart. Perhaps that's why he killed her. In the moment of her death, and the seconds before, he reacted quickly, instinctively, and without thought, but it was entirely conceivable that he'd subconsciously planned her demise long ago – when they first shared a drink at The Royale and she allowed him to touch her leg, maybe when he was first inside her, or possibly when he felt betrayed after she'd kissed her old acting teacher on the mouth. He killed her, he reasoned with himself, to keep from falling in love with her, to prevent Tammy from hurting him the same way Maggie had, to avoid another devastating blow to the heart.

Ethan wiped the water from his eyes so he could see clearly and turned the shower faucet to the right. The water stopped but the room was still humid and full of steam. He had to get out and get ready. By now, Winslow had surely counted past thirty.

•

Fresh snow began to fall from the hazy, gray sky, but it wasn't heavy enough or wet enough to prevent the windshield wipers on the truck from making that awful, rubber pressing against glass, scratching noise. The wipers had crossed the windshield only three times before Winslow decided he needed a distraction. He used just the first two preset stations on his car radio; number one was for NPR, and preset number two was locked in on FM 99.1, the classical music station. Winslow, bothered by the wipers, pressed number two, and turned up the volume. The long, slow pull of the bow across the violin strings was instantly welcomed by both he and Ethan. Neither man knew the song or its composer, but they were both filled with a sort of timeless feeling. The season's first snow was beginning gather just below blades of grass, and the classical music accentuated everything, made it eternal. The roads were still dry and there were only a few other cars out for Sunday driving so, other than the windshield wipers, things were rather peaceful. As they turned right onto Kingshighway and drove away from the tall trees of Tower Grove Park, it crossed Ethan's mind that people on horse and buggy must've once passed the same sights, the same trees – though it probably wasn't yet a park – and its passengers, quite possibly, could've had the same violin concerto running through their heads.

"You don't have to do this if you don't want to," Winslow said, stealing a peak across the cab at Ethan. "If, you know, you feel like Rach or I am pushing you or something. I mean…" He trailed off for a few beats, hoping Ethan would step in. When he didn't, he finished his thought, "You know my feelings on it is all I'm saying. It's useless if you're not ready."

Ethan was well aware of Winslow's feelings on the subject, on his commitment to the program. In fact, his nine years of sobriety and overwhelmingly positive outlook on life were driving forces for agreeing to join him at the meeting in the first place.

He looked over at Winslow, whose eyes were on the road, waiting for Ethan to speak, to assure him. "I'm good," Ethan said when he finally spoke. "I'm ready, I think I am anyway. I'm a little excited even. But I can tell you I wouldn't be going without you. There's no way in hell. So, thank you."

Winslow took his eye off the road to look over and nod his acceptance. They were on the same page and they were grateful to have each other.

Ethan turned his attention out the passenger window and tried to follow individual snowflakes as they made their way to the ground. Eventually he caught his reflection in the side mirror. For the first time in a long time, it didn't scare him. The past few weeks, since he'd first entered into sobriety, Ethan had avoided reflections. They would tear apart his insides with nausea. Each time he looked into a mirror, brushing his teeth at night or simply seeing himself in a storefront window, there was an empty skeleton staring back at him and it was terrifying. He was embarrassed with the face he'd developed, the sunken cheekbones, the yellow teeth, and his eyes looked as though they'd doubled in size. It was confusing to him. He didn't understand the radical transformation. In his mind, the post-Maggie exterior didn't represent the power and heart he felt had been beating within. The drugs had fooled him.

But now he looked better, half healthy even. Under Rachel's watchful eye, Ethan had regained his strength and pulled himself together. The color was back in his face, he'd regained the lost weight, and now he was mentally ready for a personal commitment to therapy.

Everything was more or less in place. With Rachel's help and encouragement, he'd made plans to start an aggressive job hunt in the following weeks. They were optimistic about him landing at another school for the second semester, that is if he continued to progress. After the hospital cleared him to return home, Ethan bit a massive bullet and met with Principal Fenske. He told her almost everything that had happened, (that his fiancé left him after her abortion and that those two single events were enough to send him into a mild depression) and sincerely apologized for allowing his personal life to affect the work. The truth was, he loved working with kids, helping them, and he wanted a second chance to be good at that. Fenske agreed to a letter of recommendation. He was lucky.

Objects in mirror are closer than they appear was posted on the bottom of the truck's passenger side mirror. Ethan wondered if that was true, if he was close. The mirror was curved outward to allow the driver better vision, but as Ethan stared into the reflection – his face, the road moving below, the buildings and cars – he knew the mirror couldn't begin to capture the whole story. There would always be blind spots. Nevertheless, the reflection wasn't exactly lying either. Here he was, alive, smiling even, but somewhere, if you were willing to search hard enough, you'd find the story written between the lines of his face, in his character. On some level, it was all right there on display. It just depends on the angle of the mirror, and where precisely one was looking.

The churches parking lot wasn't full but there were a dozen or so cars parked sporadically throughout. Winslow slammed the heavy truck door and took the lead. Ethan felt butterflies.

They entered Gethsemane Lutheran though the double doors just off the side of the building and walked down a wide stairwell. At the bottom of the stairwell another set of doors lead to a beautifully run down gymnasium. Ethan paused a moment to take it all in. The windows, twenty-five feet up the wall, the kind that can only be opened or closed with the help of an extended hook-pole, were open wide to allow the muggy, furnace-heated air to escape. The floor had been covered with brown tiles instead of the traditional wooden court, and there were just two rows of bleachers at mid-court. The backboards of the basketball hoops were still white and rounded at the edge, the kind made from fiberglass, not yet updated to the modern square acrylic versions seen everywhere else in the world. Ethan half expected Gene Hackman to walk out of the locker room blowing a whistle and ordering wind sprints.

There were roughly fifteen metal folding chairs around the half court circle, and while some of the seats were occupied, most were empty, waiting to provide support. Winslow put his hand on Ethan's back and escorted him to the refreshment table that had been set up along the near wall.

As they walked, Winslow shook a few hands and waved across the gym to a few more. Though he wasn't a religious man, Winslow seemed to be a regular figure here with the Gethsemane church crowd. He also carried himself in a different way, in control, with confidence. Not to say those traits weren't there before, they were, but here they were magnified. He seemed taller, friendlier, more charismatic. He could run for President. In all the years Ethan had known his brother-in-law, he suddenly felt like he'd only been acquainted with half the man. And now, here in the church gymnasium, there was so much more on display. He wondered if Rachel knew this side of Winslow, if *this* were the man she'd fallen in love with. The butterflies flapped their wings again, but now they felt like bats.

"Help yourself," Winslow said. "The chocolate long John's will rock your mind." He bit into one of the long, slender doughnuts, and with the back of his hand, wiped the pudding that spilled onto his lower lip. He continued, "Peter gets them from that little hole up the street on Lemay, the joint right next to the post office. They got the good stuff inside, not that phony icing crap that I can't stand. This is the real deal."

The table cloth was red and the paper napkins were covered in poinsettias. It was the Christmas season. As Ethan grabbed a doughnut and poured himself a cup of coffee, a pastor, dressed head to toe in black and carrying his white collar in his left hand, approached the table to strike up a conversation with Winslow.

"How's your wife, doing? The baby?" the pastor asked.

"Forget about her, she's a pro. Pregnancy's got *me* all wound up. Can't sleep, can't think. Kid's not even here yet."

Ethan watched as the two men laughed and shook hands.

"What are you, working today?" Winslow asked, gesturing to the monkey suit and collar in his hand. Ethan glanced down at the collar himself and noticed how big the pastor's hands were, especially for a man of average build. Then he looked at the bones in his own hands, protruding out as they gripped the cup of coffee. He felt small, inferior.

"Every day, brother. Every day," the big handed pastor said. "Had a funeral at Trinity cemetery this morning. Started snowing. Very poetic. But... Well, you know, it's always tough this time of year." The pastor sighed, attempting to push his sympathy aside and deal with things later. "Enough of that, though, we're here to feel good." The pastor smiled. "This the brother-in-law you told me about?"

Ethan felt smaller still. He didn't want to be talked about, didn't like the idea of it. For the past six months he'd been able to minimize the publicity surrounding everything that happened to him, and now he felt betrayed, like Winslow, or god knows who else, had spread the word, formed their own opinions, and were now silently passing their judgment upon him. He tried to shrug it off. Wins was only there to help, he told himself.

"Yes it is," Winslow said. "The man in the flesh."

"Ethan Atkinson." Ethan set the coffee down and felt his hand get swallowed up by the pastors. Somehow it still felt safe, gentle.

"Pastor Sieveking. But please call me Peter."

"Pleasure to meet you, Peter."

"Nice to meet you too, son," the pastor said. "Listen, I'm a pastor by trade, it's what's in my heart, but I'm not a pusher. You understand?"

Ethan looked over to Winslow, his grin was wide, as usual. Teeth and gums. Ethan nodded and said that he did indeed understand.

"This place, this gym, don't think of it as a church, no one's here to make you feel guilty for what's in your heart. It's not that kind of place. The next few hours are for you. Mister Winslow here told me you had some concerns about God, as does he, and I respect that. Each man has to have his own path and his own beliefs. That path lead you here, son. We're happy to have you." The pastor finally let go of Ethan's hand, and it instantly felt cold and lonely. He picked up the coffee hoping to replicate the feeling.

"Thank you, sir. Peter, I mean." The butterflies seemed to settle in the pastor's presence.

"Grab a chair, boys," the pastor said, turning to walk away. "We're gonna get started in sixty. Happy Saturday!" he said with a wink.

The circle filled quickly. Ethan got the impression that the regulars had their spots, their claimed territory, and only when sitting in their own special chair could they feel both the comfort needed to confess their sins, and the trust needed to receive support from a group of otherwise total strangers. So he hung back, finishing the doughnut – which was without question one of the best he'd ever had – until he felt safe enough to claim a chair as his own.

Winslow had saved an empty seat to his right but Ethan ignored it, choosing to sit on the opposite side of the circle. The thought of his brother-in-law patting him on the back after a "breakthrough" made him cringe. He wanted anonymous support, and in a perfect world that's what he'd get. But in a perfect world, he wouldn't need the circle to begin with. And more than anonymity, Ethan needed to apologize to Winslow eye to eye. To look across the circle and tell him how sorry he was for all he'd done wrong. If he could handle that, then later, when the time came, he could face his nephew, he could hold him and kiss him with pride instead of guilt.

Pastor Peter walked around the outside of the circle, touching a few shoulders, calming and quieting the group, until he reached the last empty chair, and placed his large paws over its back. "Two thousand years ago," Peter said in a deep, soothing voice. "Jesus turned water into wine. And most of us have been abusing it ever since. But part of being human, part of being an adult, is the ability to learn from our mistakes… to grow… to

230

hope… to trust that we can lean on others. And most importantly, to try our damnedest to make life better for those around us. Jackie Robinson was buried in Brooklyn, New York in 1972. On his headstone it says, 'A life is not important except in the impact it has on other lives.'" Peter paused and let the quote settle in among the circle. "I love that. It's one of my favorites. Myself included, we haven't always made life easier on the people who love us. The holidays are here. It's that time of year for work parties, family parties. This used to be the hardest time of year for me personally. It was always a struggle to stay clean." The pastor finally stepped into the circle from behind his chair and sat down. He made eye contact with nearly every person in the group, then continued. "Do me a favor. Look around this circle. We all come from different places, different backgrounds, and we've seen some dark things. That past got us here, looking for the light. You should applaud yourselves for having the strength to be here this afternoon. I want you to know that none of us are alone. We are growing, individually and together. Please, take the hand of the person to your left and to your right."

Ethan reached out, palms up, and took the hands of his neighbors.

"Squeeze their hands. And let's take a moment in silence, to feel one another," Peter said.

Ethan couldn't help but feel a surge of emotion run through his body. Goose bumps flared on his forearms. He wasn't sure what exactly it was he that he was feeling, it wasn't a miracle or anything fantastical, but it was a feeling. And to feel something without the aid of a drug, to be filled with a *feeling*, was infinitely better than the nothingness that had been consuming him for so long.

Pastor Peter broke the silence. "Who wants to go first?"

Ethan raised his hand.

"Good, good. Ethan is new to the group."

231

There was a wave of 'hello's' and smiles and head nods. Ethan tried to reciprocate as many as he could.

"Ethan, just... tell us what's on your mind. Tell us why you're here."

It was a strange thing, Ethan thought to himself, to start over.

Acknowledgements

First and foremost, I want to thank my beautiful wife. Without your encouragement and support I would be utterly lost. You lift me up and I love you for that; Mom, thank you for taking an active interest in my artistic life, it means the world to me; Pat, for willingly reading everything that I write and pretending it's all gold; Rob, my brother-from-another-mother, for your faith in me. A short conversation with you keeps me going; Bennett, you are the circle, thank you; Dave, for always being willing to create. Your skills will soon be recognized and I will no longer be able to afford you. Excellent work on the cover; Auggie, you're my best friend and the world's greatest listener; And finally, to the great city of St. Louis. You are a beautiful river city, and more wonderful than many people will ever know. Thank you for helping to inspire this book and also for playing a central character. You will forever be the place I call home. Go Cardinals.

About the Author

Nathan Sutton was born and raised in St. Louis county and attended Webster University. He is also the writer/director of the award winning motion picture *Autumn Wanderer*. Nathan has spent time as a bartender, waiter, construction laborer, janitor, rental car jockey, little league umpire, field maintenance worker, and occasional television actor. Nathan currently lives in Los Angeles with his wife, Elisha, and their dog, Auggie Busch Sutton II.

For more information on their work, please visit www.mohawkstreetproductions.com